Leon isn't jealous of his best friend. Really, he isn't. He doesn't do relationships, so while he's happy that Manuel has found the man of his life, he's not planning to follow down his path.

Hugh likes his life the way it is—familiar and predictable—even though most people, including his brothers, think he's boring.

He's in for the shock of his life when he meets Leon. Leon is the opposite of him. He's colorful and happy, always talking and having fun.

He's also Hugh's mate.

Hugh doesn't know what to do with that, and after Leon tells him he doesn't date, Hugh steps back, unsure whether or not he should tell Leon he's his mate.

Hugh can't keep it a secret forever, but can he ignore everything that makes him who he is and throw himself into what could be the happiest relationship of his life? And if he does, will Leon agree to take a chance, or will he run away like he's used to doing?

Opposites Attract
Copyright © 2020 Catherine Lievens
ISBN: 978-1-4874-2871-6
Cover art by Angela Waters

Published by eXtasy Books Inc or
Devine Destinies, an imprint of eXtasy Books Inc

Look for us online at:
www.eXtasybooks.com or www.devinedestinies.com

Opposites Attract
Seven Brothers Book 2

By

Catherine Lievens

CHAPTER ONE

Hugh had texted Sean before leaving his apartment, but his twin still wasn't ready. Hugh glared at the apartment building he was parked in front of and honked, even though he knew it wouldn't help. Sean would come out when he was ready, and not one second before then.

Hugh sighed and leaned back against the seat. They were going for dinner at their parents' home, and while he was always happy to see his parents and his brothers, he could have done without it today. He loved all his brothers, of course, but he didn't want to see how happy Curtis was with Manuel. It probably made him a bad brother, but he couldn't change how he felt.

"What are you doing?"

Hugh jumped in his seat and glared at Sean. "What do you think I'm doing? I thought it was obvious. I'm waiting for you."

Sean hopped into the passenger seat. "It looks like you're sleeping. Do you need to go back home? I can call Mom and tell her we're not coming."

Hugh snorted. "Sure you can. And can you also answer the dozens of questions she'll have for you?"

Sean grimaced. "She means well."

Hugh was aware of that. He loved his mom, and he loved that she wasn't nosy, but when something happened to one of her sons, she was right there in the thick of things. Mostly it was to help him get through it and support him, but she was a mother, after all, and she had questions.

A lot of them.

Hugh started the car and left Sean's building behind. Sean was humming along with the radio, and Hugh wished he'd thought about turning it off. He didn't care much about his brother singing, but Sean wasn't the best singer in the world, and his voice made Hugh cringe a few times, especially when he tried hitting high notes.

Of course, Sean noticed. "You're not a better singer than I am," he said.

"You're right. I'm not. Which is why I don't sing."

"You're boring."

Hugh cringed and prayed Sean hadn't noticed.

Boring. It was something a lot of people had told him he was, to the point that he couldn't dismiss it. Was he really boring, though?

He supposed he was. He worked from home, so he didn't go out a lot. He didn't have a lot of friends. Actually, all of his friends were his brothers, which was probably a sad thing. He spent most of his days in sweatpants, and he only went out for grocery shopping. He'd thought about getting a dog, but he still hadn't decided. Maybe it would help him leave his place, but the thought of having to walk his dog even in the rain was a bit terrifying, especially for someone who felt cold as easily as he did.

Okay. Maybe he *was* boring. What could he do about it, though? This was his life. There wasn't much to change about it.

"Hugh?"

Hugh blinked and gave Sean a quick look. "What?"

"I asked you if you knew if Curtis and Manuel will be there?"

Hugh and Sean grimaced almost at the same time. "They're supposed to be," Hugh said. "Or at least, that's what Mom said."

Sean huffed. "You know, I'm happy for Curtis and Manuel, of course, but I could do without having to watch the two of them making eyes at each other."

"They're happy. What do you want them to do?"

"I don't know, but not staring into each other's eyes as if they're alone in the world every time we're at dinner together."

Sean wasn't wrong. As happy as Hugh was for his brother, he really could do without him and his mate making googly eyes over the mashed potatoes. Of course, in Hugh's case, it was jealousy more than anything. He wanted what Curtis had, but he didn't have it. He *couldn't* have it, or at least, he didn't think so. He was pretty sure that even if he met his mate — and mates were a hard thing to come by — his mate would leave him behind because he was so boring.

"Do you want to take bets on how many times they're going to make out?"

Hugh rolled his eyes. "You can't bet on your brother."

"Why not? He and Manuel are annoying. We might as well make the most out of it and have fun."

Hugh shook his head and focused on the road. He knew Sean wasn't mean-spirited. He meant well, but he was just as annoyed as Hugh and probably most of them. Hugh doubted their younger brothers cared about meeting their mates, but eventually, they might. They were young, though. Laurie was only nineteen, so why would he want to meet his mate now? But Hugh and Sean were thirty-five, and Richie twenty-seven. Hugh didn't know how Richie felt about Curtis and Manuel, but he knew what *he* felt, and it wasn't good. He might be happy for his brother, but he hated feeling jealous and like Curtis had gotten something before he had. He realized it was the big brother part of him talking when he thought that, but it didn't help.

He was both relieved and annoyed when he finally parked

in front of their parents' home. The last thing he wanted was to have dinner with Curtis and Manuel cooing over each other, but there was no way out of its. Their mom wanted them home every Sunday evening, so that was what they did.

Sean disappeared inside the house before Hugh had a chance to get out of the car. He was probably hungry, and while Hugh followed him, it was at a more sedate pace. He closed the front door behind himself and briefly closed his eyes, soaking in the familiarity of everything. The smells, the voices, everything reminded him of his childhood.

He headed to the kitchen, surprised to see Curtis there with their mom and Manuel nowhere to be seen. "Where did you leave your better half?" he asked as he stole a piece of carrot from the plate his mom had put together. She tried to smack his hand with a wooden spoon, but he was too fast. He'd been doing this for thirty-five years, after all.

Curtis grinned at him. "He *is* my better half, isn't he?"

"I wouldn't have said that otherwise. So? Where is he? Did you abandon him with everyone else in the living room? You know they're going to send him running if you leave him alone with them."

"He's back home. I think he wanted to move some stuff so he could make space for mine."

Right. Because Curtis was moving in with his mate. "So you're doing it, then?" Hugh asked.

"Of course I'm doing it. I can't wait."

Hugh laughed. "You can't wait to leave this house, you mean?"

This time, the wooden spoon smacked him right on the hand. "What are you trying to say?" his mom asked.

Hugh grimaced and rubbed his hand. "Nothing bad. But come on, Mom. He's thirty-two. Of course he wants to leave the house and stop living with his parents."

"I'll have you know that we didn't force him to stay. He's

an adult. He can leave whenever he wants."

"I never said you did. Come on, Mom. I wasn't trying to say a bad thing." Hugh was happy to see Curtis moving on after he'd broken up with his former boyfriend. He'd had to move back to their parents' home for a bit, but now that was over. Curtis was starting his future with Manuel, and Hugh would be right there to watch while he did.

"You'll help me, then?" Curtis asked.

Hugh blinked. "Help you?"

"With the move. There's not a lot, since I left most of my furniture behind when I moved back here, and Manuel already has all of that anyway, but I do have several boxes and a little furniture."

Hugh wanted to say no. He loved his brothers, but spending any length of time with them was draining, and even though Curtis claimed not to have a lot to move, Hugh knew it would take them a while. He couldn't say no, though. "Sure. Just let me know when, and I'll be there."

Curtis grinned and clapped Hugh's back. "Thanks. I don't know what I'd do if you left me alone with the kids."

Hugh snorted. "I doubt Laurie will show up, whatever he's told you."

"True. He'll probably be too busy with his current boy-friend. Or is it a girlfriend? I've lost count."

God, Hugh's brothers were irritating. He wouldn't have it any other way, though. They were his brothers, and he loved them — more than he liked himself, most of the time.

Leon rolled on his stomach and looked at Manuel. He couldn't remember the last time he'd seen his best friend behaving this way. Manuel was checking his reflection in the mirror, even though he already knew that Curtis, his boy-friend, was a sure thing. "You know he's not going to care even if your hair isn't perfect," Leon pointed out.

Manuel looked at him through the mirror. "I know. I still want to be perfect for him."

Leon sighed. He wanted to look perfect for someone, too. He knew better than to expect or hope that he would ever have what Manuel had with Curtis, though. "Tell me about his family." Leon was curious, both about Curtis and his family. Curtis had six brothers, and that wasn't something Leon had experience with.

Manuel smiled. "They're all great. The younger brothers are a bit weird, but I think that's because they're not sure what to make of me. They're all single, you know? I'm the first serious relationship any of them has had, or at least, the first serious relationship they know is going to last."

Leon frowned. "No offense, but how can they know you and Curtis will last?"

Manuel shrugged. "I know. I mean, I'm not going anywhere, and neither is Curtis. That has to mean something, right? I can feel it. He's the guy for me, and I'm not about to do anything that can jeopardize our future."

Leon narrowed his eyes, but even though he knew Manuel was hiding something from him, he didn't ask. When and if Manuel was ready to tell him about it, he would be there. In the meantime, he didn't mind listening to what Curtis' brothers were up to.

He couldn't help but think about Manuel going to Sunday dinner with all those guys. Of course, Manuel only had eyes for Curtis. But Leon wanted to meet the other brothers, too. Were they as hot as Curtis? There was bound to be least one or two of them who weren't, but Curtis was damn sexy, and Leon wondered if maybe one of his brothers might be the man for him.

But no. He already knew the answer to that question. Meeting them wouldn't change it.

"And they welcomed you okay?" he asked.

Manuel smiled. "Yeah. You could come along, if you want. I'm sure Curtis's mother won't mind. I mean, she already has to feed eight men and herself, and you eat like a bird. It wouldn't change anything for her."

It was tempting to say yes. Leon couldn't remember the last time he'd had a home-cooked meal. He certainly wasn't one for cooking, which meant that he usually survived on sandwiches and take-out. He also wanted to spend more time with Manuel. Now that Manuel had Curtis, it felt like they didn't see each other often enough.

But he knew better than to accept the invitation. Parents didn't like him. He knew why, and he wasn't about to change, but he didn't want Manuel to be offended or disappointed. Manuel liked Curtis and his family, and from the way things were going, Leon suspected he would be part of that family for a long time. Hell, Curtis was already moving in with him, and they'd only known each other for a few months.

Things between Manuel and Curtis were serious, and while Leon was happy for his best friend, he also couldn't help but feel like he was losing him in a way. "I can't come, but if you want, I can help with the move."

Manuel snorted. "You mean you'll keep an eye on Curtis's brothers while they move his stuff?"

Leon grinned. "Of course. Isn't that what I just said?"

Manuel turned around and leaned against the dresser. "I'll be happy to have your help. Curtis doesn't have a lot of stuff, though. I doubt there'll be much for you to do, considering he has six brothers. But of course you're welcome to come."

Leon grinned and sat up, crossing his legs under himself. "I wouldn't miss it for anything. Like you said, he has six brothers. If they're anything like him, I can't wait to watch them work." He wiggled his eyebrows so Manuel would know what he was talking about.

Manuel shook his head, amused. "They're all single as far as I know."

"Oh, I'm not looking for anyone to fill my bed, don't worry."

Manuel frowned, and Leon knew he shouldn't have said that. He'd been trying to hide how lonely he was from his best friend for a while, and he wasn't doing a good job, especially not since Curtis had appeared in the picture. Leon was distracted, which meant that he needed to be more careful. He didn't want Manuel to worry about him. He didn't want *anyone* to worry about him.

He did enough worrying on his own.

"Are you sure you don't want to come?" Manuel asked.

Leon shook his head. "I'm sure. They're your family. You should spend time with them."

"You're my family, too. You *can* come. I told you they wouldn't mind. If anything, they'll be happy to meet you. I might have mentioned you a few times, and Curtis knows you."

Leon shook his head and reached for his shoes on the floor. "I'll go home. I have things to do."

"Things to do? Like what?"

Leon looked at Manuel. He knew his friend didn't believe him, but that was okay. As long as Leon could continue faking, everything would be fine. "Well, I need to do my nails. I'm not crazy about this color I chose last time."

"And you can't do that another day?"

Leon huffed and crossed his arms over his chest, glaring at Manuel. "What do you want from me? I told you I don't want to come. Are you going to force me?"

Manuel jerked back, and Leon felt instantly guilty. He hated pushing his best friend away. He knew Manuel was only badgering him because he cared and worried. That didn't make it easier to deal with, though. Leon understood where Manuel was coming from, and he was grateful to have his best friend in his life, but right now, he wanted to be alone.

He knew that if he pushed, Manuel would eventually give up and leave him behind. That wasn't what Leon wanted, though. He loved Manuel, albeit not in the same way Curtis loved him. But Leon knew he was weird. He knew he was defective, and he only had Manuel in his life. Maybe it would be better for everyone if Manuel stepped out of it, but Leon couldn't bring himself to push his only friend away.

He cleared his throat. "Maybe I'll go to a bar or something. I might find some company."

"Leon—"

Leon shook his head again. "No. I know you want me to be part of your family, and I'm grateful for it. I love you. You know that. But I can't have what you and Curtis have, and that's okay. I need you to stop pushing, though."

"I don't understand why you think you can't have it. I know you like using guys and throwing them away like dirty tissues, and that's fine. It's never been my thing, but I don't have anything against it, if that's what you enjoy. I'm just not sure you're still enjoying it."

Leon rubbed his face, careful of his eyes. He didn't want to smudge his mascara or the dark eyeliner around his eyes. "I know you don't understand, and I don't need you to. I just need you to support me. Please."

"Of course I'll support you. I wish I could do more, though."

"There's nothing to do." Leon got to his feet and forced himself to smile. "I'm fine. I promise. You'll be the first one to know if that changes, but right now, you should focus on Curtis. The two of you haven't been together long, and I can't believe he's moving in with you already," Leon said.

Leon was slightly worried. This wasn't like Manuel, and he couldn't help but wonder if maybe losing his mom was still hitting Manuel as hard as it had in the beginning. He wanted to do something, but he knew it would be hard. Manuel hadn't lost just anyone. He'd lost his mom, and that would leave traces for a long time. Maybe finding Curtis was the best thing that could have happened to him. Leon still wished things hadn't changed between them, but he understood how ridiculous that thought was.

Manuel had Curtis now. He might not want to leave Leon behind, but Leon needed to start living without Manuel at his side.

The problem was that he wasn't sure he could.

Hugh was pretty sure he was the only one who heard the knock on the door, so he pushed away from the counter, left his mom and his brothers to the cooking, and went to open it.

Manuel was standing there, and he smiled as soon as he saw Hugh. There was no way Hugh could hold anything against him. Manuel was a sweet man, and he made Curtis happy.

Hugh smiled back at him. "Hey. Curtis was just saying he wasn't sure you were coming. I think he said something about you making space for him in your house."

Manuel rolled his eyes. "I told him I *was* coming. Sometimes, I can't believe that man."

Hugh laughed. "I think we're on the same page there. I've known him for thirty-two years, but he's still impossible sometimes."

Manuel stepped inside, and Hugh closed the door behind him. He watched Manuel as he took off his coat and hung it. It was as if he belonged here just as much as Hugh, and Hugh realized that was the case. Manuel and Curtis hadn't been together long, but they were mates, and that meant a lot. It meant that Manuel wasn't going anywhere. It meant that he was family now, and nothing would ever change that.

Hugh was used to having six brothers, but now he had seven, and that was going to take some time to wrap his mind around.

"So you've already made space for Curtis' stuff?" he asked as he and Manuel headed to the kitchen.

Dinner wasn't ready yet, but Hugh's mom liked having her sons help her. She could do all of this of her own, of course, but none of them wanted her to. It was Sunday dinner, which meant it was an occasion for all of them to be together. Cooking as a group helped with that, although Hugh could have done without Laurie almost setting fire to the salad earlier. Hugh wasn't even sure how he'd managed, and he didn't want to find out. It was a small miracle that Laurie was still alive, although the fact that he still lived with their parents probably helped. He was only nineteen anyway. He had all the time in the world to learn how to cook and how not to set the kitchen on fire when he did.

Manuel made a beeline for Curtis, of course, and Curtis's expression lit up. It was like someone turned on the light, and Hugh couldn't feel resentful for that. He might be jealous, and he might want what Curtis and Manuel had, but he was happy for his brother.

He couldn't help but watch the two as they said hello. Manuel's cheeks were slightly flushed, but he didn't seem to care that everyone was staring at him. It would take some time for the family to get used to having him around. Curtis was the first of the seven brothers to find his mate, and that was a joyous occasion. It was also strange for the family to change this way, though. A few of them had brought home boyfriends or girlfriends, but none had been as serious as finding your mate was. All those relationships had failed eventually, but the one between Curtis and Manuel wouldn't.

They were mates, so that was a guarantee, although of

course, one of them could fuck things up. Hugh would bet on Curtis doing that eventually, but from what he knew of the two, he was pretty sure Manuel would forgive him almost everything.

"Manuel!" Hugh's mom said. "Curtis was saying he wasn't sure you were coming."

Manuel shook his head. "I didn't have to move that much stuff to make space for him. I mean, he only has a few boxes and some furniture. I'm not even sure why he wants his brothers to help him move."

Hugh smiled. He suspected he knew the answer to that. Curtis' life was changing. It had already changed a lot when he'd broken up with his last boyfriend and moved back home to live with their parents. He got teased for that by most of their brothers, but Hugh never brought it up. He could imagine how hard everything was for Curtis, and the fact that he had retreated to their parents' home meant he'd been hurting. But now he'd found Manuel, and his life was changing again. He was moving in with his mate. He was happy, and that much was evident to anyone who looked at him and Manuel. Hugh suspected he wanted his brothers there when he took that next step.

Hugh would be more than happy to help. Curtis, and of course Sean, were the two brothers he was closest to. It was probably because they were close in age and they'd grown up together. Hugh loved all of his brothers, but he was already thirty-five, while Laurie, the youngest, was only nineteen. It was a huge age difference, and some days, Laurie felt more like he was Hugh's kid that his sibling.

Hugh was grateful he wasn't, though. He didn't have to deal with all the one-night stands Laurie brought home.

Curtis laughed and hooked his arm around Manuel's shoulders to pull him close. Watching them together made Hugh wonder if he would ever meet his mate. And if he did, would his mate like him? He knew his life was okay, but not exciting, and he wasn't sure he could change that.

The thought terrified him. What if he found his mate, told him what they were to each other, and his mate pushed him away? What if his mate didn't want anything to do with him?

"Hugh? Is everything okay?" Curtis asked.

Hugh forced himself to smile even though he didn't feel like it. "Of course. Mom? Is there anything I can take to the dining room?"

It was easy to lose himself in his family after that. Now that Manuel was part of it, there were ten of them around the table, and that made for a lot of noise and several conversations. No one noticed that Hugh kept to himself and stayed silent. They were used to it. Hugh had always been quiet, and that would never change. Hugh didn't *want* to change. He might be boring, but he liked his life. He liked how predictable and dependable it was. He didn't want surprises. He wanted to know what would happen to him every minute of every day. And if that meant his mate didn't want him, then it was okay with him.

Or at least, that was what he was trying to convince himself of.

He ran to the kitchen as soon as they were done eating. Their mom had cooked, which meant they were on cleanup duty. Hugh didn't mind staying in the kitchen to rinse plates and glasses and put them in the dishwasher. He worked on his own, smiling and nodding at his brothers when they brought in the dirty dishes. They disappeared into the living room once that was done, and Hugh relaxed. He should have known better, though.

Curtis walked into the kitchen, holding the last plates. He put them next to the sink, but he didn't leave like the others had. Instead, he crossed his arms over his chest and leaned against the counter. Hugh did his best to ignore him, but no one could ignore Curtis. Still, he focused on the dishes and acted as if his brother wasn't there until Curtis had enough.

"What's going on with you?" Curtis finally asked.

Hugh shook his head. "Nothing. I'm just trying to finish this so I can go home. You know I like to go to bed early." One more sign that he was boring, probably.

"You're lying."

Hugh straightened and stared at his brother. "How do you know I'm lying? I'm not," he added, just in case.

Hugh knew his reaction to seeing Curtis and Manuel together was stupid. He didn't want to talk to Curtis about it. He didn't want to hurt Curtis, and that was what would happen if he did.

"Come on, Hugh. You don't have to hide things from me. I know I've been more distant since I've met Manuel, but I'm still your brother."

Hugh rubbed his forehead. He wasn't going to win this, was he?

"It's nothing. You should go to Manuel."

"I will, but first, I want to know what's going on with you. And don't say it's nothing again. I can tell that's not the case."

Hugh wished he could get out of this conversation, but he knew better. "It's *nothing*. I'm a bit jealous when I see you and Manuel, but that's it. I'm happy for you. I'm feeling sorry for myself, but it'll pass. It always does."

Curtis frowned. "I get it, but I don't like that you feel that way."

"It has nothing to do with you. I promise. Now get your mate and spend some time with him. That's why he's here after all."

Curtis looked like he wanted to protest, but thankfully, he didn't, and Hugh went back to the dishes until his brother was gone. He couldn't help how he felt about seeing Curtis and Manuel together, but he could make sure his brother didn't get hurt over his feelings. Curtis deserved to be happy, and Hugh wouldn't do anything to ruin that.

Leon admired his now red nails. He wasn't quite sure about the color, but he liked it. It would make people look at him, but then what was new about that? People always thought he was weird. That wasn't going to change anytime soon, whatever color his nails were.

His phone rang, and he swore. He hoped he wasn't going to ruin his nails. He wasn't up for doing them all over again. He was careful as he tapped on the screen with his fingertips, answering his mom's phone call. "I'm doing my nails," he said as a hello.

"That means you can talk, right?" his mom asked.

Leon rolled his eyes. She wouldn't take no for an answer, would she? "Yep. I can talk if you need me to."

"I wouldn't call you if I didn't want to talk to you. What's going on?"

Leon closed his eyes. His mom knew him better than anyone except maybe Manuel. There was no way he could hide anything from her, although perhaps, since they were on the phone, it would be easier. "Nothing is going on with me. What about you? Anything new to tell me?"

There was a pause, then, instead of answering, she asked, "What about Manuel? Don't you spend Sunday evenings together usually? I thought I'd catch him if I called you now."

"He's with his boyfriend and the guy's family."

"Curtis! How is he? Why aren't you with them? And don't tell me Manuel didn't ask you to go with them. I know that boy. I'm sure he did."

Sometimes, Leon *hated* how well his mom knew him. "Of course he invited me. I declined."

"Why? Curtis has six brothers, doesn't he? Maybe you can

15

snatch one of them."

Leon had to roll his eyes at that. "We already talked about that, Mom. Stop trying to make me hook up and find a boyfriend."

"I want you to be happy. I want you to have what Manuel and Curtis have."

Leon wished his mom hadn't met Curtis. She'd gone to Manuel's house to leave him something to eat the way she'd started doing after Manuel's mom died, and Curtis had been there. Leon hadn't been, but he'd heard all about their meeting, and he knew she was delighted by the man Manuel had found. But it meant that now she was on the warpath for Leon to find himself a man, too.

She, more than anyone, should know why he didn't have anyone important in his life, but he wasn't about to bring it up. He didn't want to fight with her, not when he already felt lonely.

"I'm fine with my life how it is," he told her.

"But Curtis is a nice man."

"I know. He's the perfect man for Manuel. I'm not into that kind of relationship, though. You know that." Leon was okay with his one-night stands, or at least, so he tried to convince himself.

He suspected his mom knew as well as he did that it wasn't true. He was grateful she didn't say it, though.

He knew he wouldn't have what Manuel and Curtis had. He'd tried a few times in the past, and it hadn't ended well. He wasn't about to try again. He couldn't, not when every time it felt like his heart had been torn out of his chest.

"When's the last time you had a boyfriend?" his mom asked.

Dammit. He'd thought he was safe from that. "I don't know. I don't have time for a boyfriend. I don't want one. I'm happy Manuel found what he was looking for, but it's not for me, Mom. I need you to stop asking. Please." Because every time she did, it hurt. Every time she asked, it reminded Leon of what he was missing in his life.

"All right. Tell me something else, then. I want to hear about your life."

Leon didn't want to talk about his life. He was happy to hear from his mom, but he needed some time to himself. He sighed. He knew better than to try to avoid her. "There's nothing new. Just the same old stuff."

"I worry about you."

There it was again. Leon knew she meant well. He was grateful for it, too. He loved his mom, and she loved him. A lot of people in her situation would have chosen his dad over him, but she hadn't. She'd been there for Leon for the past twenty-seven years. She'd been there with him even when he thought he was alone, when his dad had decided he didn't love him anymore.

But he wasn't stupid. He knew that what had happened with his father had colored the way he saw life now and that it always would. He didn't want to talk about it, though.

"I started painting again," he told her to distract her.

He could hear the smile in her voice as she spoke. "You have? That's great. It's been a while, hasn't it?"

"It has. I've been too busy to do much of anything." Leon wrote for blogs and whatnot, which meant he worked for himself. He loved the freedom that writing freelance offered him, but he felt like he was always working, and like he had zero time to do things he loved, like painting.

He wasn't a great painter, but it helped him. It made him feel better. It settled his heart like nothing else did. But working for himself meant that he had the freedom to be just the way he was, with his nail polish, makeup, and everything else, and he didn't want it to stop.

"Your father called me," his mom said.

That was enough to make Leon freeze. He didn't care if his nails got ruined anymore, and he held the phone closer to his ear. "What did he want?"

She sighed heavily. "He said he misses me."

Leon snorted. "Tough shit. Did you tell him to fuck off.?"

"I did."

But there was something there, something she wasn't telling him. "Please tell me you're not thinking about going back to him." Leon wasn't sure he could survive that, not after what had happened.

"Of course not. After what he did to you, I'm never seeing him again."

"You should block his number. He doesn't deserve you, Mom." Leon could never forget the fact that she'd had to choose between her husband and her son, and that she'd chosen Leon. It meant a lot to him. It always had. Still, she'd lost a lot.

"I am *not* going back to him," she said, her voice stronger.

"You miss him, don't you?"

"It's complicated. But I am never going back. I promise you that. I don't care how much in love I was with him, or how happy I was. The day he kicked you out of the house was the day everything was over with him. That isn't going to change."

"Maybe he's different now." Leon wasn't sure why he was saying that. He didn't think his father was any different. He was a loser. He probably needed money, or maybe he hoped Leon's mom had forgotten what he'd done, or at the very least, forgiven him. Leon prayed his mom would see right through it, but he wasn't about to tell her how to live our life.

"It's hard because of everything I lost, but I don't regret for one second choosing you. I would do it all over again if I had to. I shouldn't have answered the call."

"No. You did well. I want to know if he's reaching out." If

anything, because that way, Leon could be sure to avoid him. He never wanted to see his father again. As far as he was concerned, he didn't have a father anymore.

"You're my son. You shouldn't have to live through this kind of thing."

"I love you, Mom." He needed her to know. He needed her to realize that even though she'd lost a lot, she hadn't lost him.

"I know. I love you, too. And forget about your father. I don't know why he called, and I don't care. Whatever he wants, he won't find it with me."

Leon wished he could be as sure as she was. Even though he didn't want to see his father, he couldn't help but wonder what was happening with him. Why was he calling now, after all this time? He had to know Leon's mom was still with him. That was why she'd left him in the first place. That hadn't changed, and Leon prayed it wouldn't.

He had so few people in his life. His mom, and of course, Manuel. It was easy to imagine what would happen if he lost either of them. But maybe his father's unexpected reappearance in his life meant that he had to start thinking about that.

CHAPTER TWO

Hugh wasn't looking forward to spending time with his brothers, but it was moving day. Curtis was officially leaving their parents' house to move in with Manuel, and Hugh, just like their other brothers, had offered to help him. Hugh had thought Curtis would refuse, considering how few things he had to move, but of course, Curtis had agreed. He'd actually seemed excited about it, and Hugh didn't understand it, especially after the conversation they'd had in the kitchen.

Hugh had admitted that he was jealous of his younger brother and that he wanted what Curtis had. He'd admitted that when he looked at Curtis and Manuel, he felt bad. He'd thought for sure that Curtis would want to give them space, if anything so Hugh wouldn't bother him in the honeymoon stage of his relationship. Instead, Curtis was acting as if Hugh hadn't said anything. He didn't seem bothered, and it puzzled Hugh, although maybe it shouldn't. He knew Curtis and how easy-going Curtis was.

"Where are Jack and Andy?" Sean asked.

"No clue. They texted me to say they were coming, but I haven't heard from them since," Curtis said. "And Richie can't come at all."

"Laurie?"

Curtis shrugged. "He's probably still in bed with his latest boyfriend or girlfriend."

That wasn't something Hugh wanted to think about. "What do we do then? Do we start without them?" he asked.

"I don't see why not."

Hugh huffed and grabbed one of the many boxes that were labeled with Curtis' name in their parents' garage. Of course Jack and Andy were late. When weren't they? He wasn't surprised they were avoiding the work, even though they'd said they were coming, just like he wouldn't be surprised if Laurie didn't show up at all.

He moved the box to the van Curtis had rented and pushed it as deep inside as he could. Once he was done, he went back inside the garage to grab another one. That seemed to be the signal for his brothers to start helping. Sean mirrored Hugh's moves, grabbing boxes and putting them in the van. They were lucky Curtis didn't have a lot of stuff, but still, it was more than Hugh had expected.

"How many trips do you think we'll have to make?" he asked Curtis when they crossed paths.

Curtis shrugged. "Not many. There are more boxes than I remembered, but the van is big."

"I thought you left a lot more stuff with your ex," Sean pointed out.

Hugh glared at him. It was never a good thing to bring up Curtis' ex. Usually, Curtis closed himself off when the topic came up, but Hugh shouldn't have been surprised that Curtis didn't react the same way this time. After all, he'd found his mate and was moving in with him. That had to beat any memory Sean's words had brought up.

Curtis chuckled. "I did leave a lot of stuff behind, but I also brought a lot more stuff than I expected. What did you think? That you weren't going to have to work? You volunteered to help."

"Only because Mom would have my ass if I hadn't. You know how she is. You're the first of her sons to find his mate. She's over the moon."

Curtis' smile widened. "Can you blame her? None of you guys have anyone in your lives. I don't think she considers

Laurie's boyfriends and girlfriends anyone she wants to meet. Manuel is the only one who's here to stay for now."

That much was true. But then, Laurie was only nineteen, so he had more than enough time to settle down, if that was what he wanted. He was very vocal when it came to the fact that he didn't want to meet his mate and that he didn't like the thought of someone else deciding for him who he would spend the rest of his life with, but Hugh suspected that would eventually change. He remembered that Curtis and Sean weren't overly happy about the thought of meeting their mates when they were younger, but now? He was happy to have found Manuel, as it should be.

They filled the van until nothing else fit, then they climbed inside and headed to Manuel's house. Hugh wasn't looking forward to seeing him, and he felt guilty about it. He liked Manuel. He thought Manuel was the best man possible for Curtis, which was normal since they were mates. But even if they hadn't been, Hugh would have liked Manuel for Curtis. They fit well together. They were happy, and that was all that mattered. That didn't help Hugh feel less jealous, though. Maybe coming hadn't been a good idea after all, but it was too late to do anything about it.

Curtis parked in front of Manuel's house, and the door flung open. Manuel stood there, bouncing on the balls of his feet, grinning from ear to ear. He was happy to see Curtis, and his expression caused a twinge of pain in Hugh's chest.

Of course they were excited. They were moving in together, and they were in love. Manuel even knew that Curtis was a swan shifter. He'd been shocked in the beginning, but he was still there, and that was important.

Curtis climbed out of the van and made a beeline for his mate. Hugh and Sean hung back, waiting for Manuel and Curtis to say hello.

"I bet you fifty dollars that they go over fifty public kisses today," Sean murmured.

Hugh reached out and gently slapped the back of his brother's head. "Don't bet on your brothers."

Sean grinned. "God, sometimes when you open your mouth, I could swear Mom is speaking."

"That's a disturbing image I didn't need."

"Then stop sounding like her. Live a little. Have fun. It's not like I'm doing this to be mean or anything. I'm happy for them. I just wish they didn't make out as much as they do when we're there."

"What did you expect? They're mates. They're moving in together. They're going to make out." And Hugh was *not* going to bet how many times they would kiss. He didn't want to think of his brother in that kind of situation.

He climbed out of the van, leaving Sean behind. Curtis and Manuel were still talking, their heads close together, but Hugh ignored them and went to open the back of the van. He took out one of the boxes and turned, almost colliding with Manuel. "Sorry," Manuel said, stumbling back. "I just wanted to help."

"You don't have to. We have it in hand, don't worry."

Manuel was still smiling. "I'm sure you do, but still. I don't want to watch you work. Besides, I managed to get someone to help. Well, help might be a big word for what Leon will do, but he's here anyway."

Manuel grabbed one of the boxes and followed Hugh inside the house. "Who's Leon?" Hugh asked to make conversation. He always felt awkward when he was with Manuel, and it wasn't Manuel's fault. It was Hugh's. He was always awkward in social situations, and unfortunately, that included situations in which Manuel was present.

"He's my best friend. I thought I'd already told you about him."

"You probably did. I don't remember, though, sorry."

"It's okay. Leon's my best friend. He agreed to help, although I'm not sure how much help he's going to be. He doesn't like to get his hands dirty."

"Are you talking about me?" a voice asked from the kitchen.

Hugh looked up just in time to see a very colorful gorgeous man step out of the kitchen. His hair was pink, and a small ring glinted in his nose. He was wearing eyeliner, and unless Hugh was mistaken, lipstick. He wasn't very tall, and he was thin, almost willowy.

And he was the most beautiful man Hugh had ever seen.

Leon beamed at the sight of Manuel standing with a man he didn't know. He suspected the guy was one of Curtis' brothers, and it made Leon think there had to be something weird in the water around here. He hadn't met all the brothers yet, but how could they be so gorgeous? Leon didn't know, and right now, he didn't care.

He beamed at the man. "Well, hello there, gorgeous. I'm Leon."

The man blinked. "I'm Hugh. Curtis' older brother."

Leon batted his lashes. "Older? You don't look older."

"That's because I'm only three years older. Well, my twin brother and I are."

There were *two* of them? Leon wasn't sure he would survive the day. "I'm sure you are the most gorgeous of the two."

Hugh cocked his head. "We're twins. We're identical."

Leon wasn't quite sure what to do with that. He was grateful when Curtis walked in and turned his attention toward his best friend's boyfriend. "Curtis! I missed you so much."

Curtis rolled his eyes. "Leon. I thought Manuel was lying when he said you were coming."

"Of course not. I had to help. Even though I have to admit,

I'm jealous of Manuel. He managed to snag himself a man like you, while poor little old me is all alone."

"You can't tell me you're here to help, though. I know you, even though not that well. I'm sure you don't want to break a nail or something."

Leon stuck his tongue out at Curtis. "You're no fun." He wasn't wrong, though.

Curtis was fun, and Leon was flirting with him because he knew Curtis wasn't available. He was safe. Besides, he liked that Curtis flirted right back and that Manuel didn't care. He would have said something if he did, but instead, he was watching them and smiling.

"Anyway," Leon said. "Since I'm here to help, I can direct you two where to put the boxes. What are you holding?"

Curtis looked down. "Looks like I have some pans and stuff like that."

Leon stepped aside and gestured toward the kitchen. "You know where those things go."

"Oh, I don't know what I would do without your help."

When Curtis passed by Leon, Leon smacked his ass. He looked at Manuel and Curtis to make sure they were okay, but both of them were laughing, and Leon relaxed. Maybe he was pushing a bit, but he felt awkward, and he wasn't quite sure what else to do. He could still feel Hugh watching him, and he didn't know why. He also wasn't sure he wanted to find out.

Leon knew that if he was going to stay in Manuel's life — and he was planning to — he would have to get used to being around Curtis and his brothers. He might as well start now. It was hard, because he wasn't used to having this many people around, but he could do it, and if he couldn't, he could fake his way through it.

The front door swung open again, and two more men walked in. Leon beamed at them. "More brothers!" he said, clapping his hands together.

The two new arrivals were Jack and Andy. Leon had made sure to ask Manuel who was who, so he remembered the order in which the brothers were born. He hadn't needed Hugh to tell him about his twin brother. If there was something to know about the family, Leon had probably already heard it from Manuel.

Jack and Andy were fun, and they were closer to Leon's age. He talked to them as they worked, coming and going from inside the house to the van parked outside, unloading boxes and a few pieces of furniture they went back to pick up. Leon stayed right where he was in the entrance, directing everyone and laughing at Jack and Andy's jokes. He stayed away from the twins, although he wasn't quite sure why. Sean and Hugh were nice men, but Hugh especially was Leon's type, and he knew better than to get close to him.

Hugh was an odd mix of awkwardness and sweetness. Even though Leon didn't know him, he could imagine what being with him could be like. Leon couldn't afford to be in a relationship, though. He couldn't afford to have his heart broken. He was okay on his own, and that wasn't about to change. He didn't want to face rejection, so it was better if he stayed away from Hugh. Still, he couldn't help that his gaze drifted his way a few times.

Hugh was his type in more ways than one. He and Sean were identical twins, about six foot two, with brown hair that curled around their ears. Sean's was shorter, and while his cut was a good one, Leon found himself wanting to tug on Hugh's slightly too-long hair. He couldn't help but imagine how that would feel in bed, possibly with Hugh's mouth on his skin.

But no. He needed to stop thinking about that. He couldn't afford to feel anything for anyone, but least of all the people who were now Manuel's family. Leon didn't want to ruin things for his friend, and that meant keeping his eyes and his hands away from Hugh.

It was hard, though. Leon tried to focus on something else, but he found his gaze drifting to Hugh every so often anyway. He was pretty sure no one noticed, which was a good thing.

"So, Leon, what do you do?" Jack asked.

Leon cocked his hip and put his hand onto it. "Wouldn't you like to know?"

Jack laughed. "I wouldn't have asked if I didn't want to."

"I'm a freelance writer."

"You don't sound enthusiastic about it."

"Let's just say it pays the bills, but no, I'm not enthusiastic."

"Leon is an artist," Manuel intervened.

Leon glared at him. "It's a hobby, and I am *far* from being an artist."

"That's because you don't paint often. It would be great if you could do that for a living."

Leon rolled his eyes. "You know that's never going to happen. Now, how much stuff is still in the van?"

Manual arched a brow. "Why? Are you planning to go out there and grab a box? Because I don't think I've seen you do anything but talk since you arrived."

Leon wiggled his fingers in Manuel's face. "You wouldn't want me to ruin my manicure, would you? Do you know how long it took me to have these perfect nails?"

Manuel shook his head and kissed Leon's cheek. "I have no idea, and I don't want to find out. But stay here. I'm glad for your presence, but I don't want you to hurt yourself by picking up a box."

Leon knew Manuel meant it. He truly didn't care that Leon wasn't working and was flirting with Curtis and his brothers. That was why he was Leon's best friend. He accepted Leon the way he was, and he knew Leon wasn't serious with the flirting.

Although if he had a chance, Leon would be deadly serious about Hugh.

Leon turned Hugh's way again. He and his twin brother were talking, and a smile was playing on Hugh's lips. Leon wanted to know what was making him smile so he could say or do it again and again until Hugh never stopped smiling.

Dammit. Leon couldn't afford this. He couldn't afford to feel anything for any of Curtis' brothers. It wasn't his fault that all of them were gorgeous, though. It *was* probably his fault that he found Hugh so appealing, though, but he didn't know what to do about it. He wasn't sure there was anything he could do except stay away, so that was what he tried to do as well as he could, even though it felt like a part of his heart shriveled in his chest.

Hugh was intrigued by Leon, but he knew better. Leon was everything he wasn't. He was beautiful and fun, and he wasn't even looking at Hugh, who was boring and old, at least next to Leon. It was better if Hugh kept his distance, but he was finding it hard.

He wasn't sure what it was about Leon. He was beautiful, with his makeup and colored hair and clothes. But even with all of that, he was just a guy. He seemed like he was a good friend to Manuel and maybe Curtis, so maybe that was what was so intriguing about him. Hugh didn't have friends, only his brothers. He didn't know what he would do with a friend, but Leon didn't seem to have trouble.

While Hugh focused on moving things out of the van and into the house, he couldn't ignore the way Leon was laughing and flirting with his brothers. He hated that he felt a pang of jealousy deep in his stomach. He didn't have a say in who Leon flirted with. It was obvious he preferred Hugh's brothers to Hugh, and who could blame him? Hugh certainly didn't. He would prefer his brothers' presence to his any day, too.

"He's looking at you," Sean said, elbowing Hugh in the ribs.

Hugh shook his head and put down the box he'd been holding. He was making a neat pile, but he needed to start a new one before this one toppled over. "I don't know what you're talking about."

"Of course you do. Leon, Manuel's friend. He's looking at you."

Hugh didn't turn to check. "He's flirting with Jack and Andy."

"Well, yes, but it looks to me like it's more habit than because he's interested in them. I'm telling you. He's looking at you."

Hugh shook his head. "There are more boxes in the van."

He ignored Sean's frown and went back outside. Right now, he seemed to be the only one working, but that was okay. It gave him something to do. If there was one thing he hated, it was having to hang around not doing anything and looking awkward.

He wasn't good at conversations. He wasn't good at making friends or being social. That was one of the reasons he worked from home. Or maybe, the fact that he worked from home was one of the reasons he was like this. He didn't know, and at this point, he didn't care. He was happy the way he was, or at least, mostly happy. He couldn't deny that he was jealous and lonely, but he would get over it. He would have to. He didn't want to continue feeling this way.

"I wasn't joking," Sean said, following Hugh outside.

Hugh wished Sean would drop it, but he knew better. His brother was stubborn, almost as much as he was. Almost, because when they fought, Sean always thought he was in the right, and Hugh would have to apologize even though he didn't feel like it. It was the only way for him to make peace with his brother, and most of the time, it was worth it.

"So? Maybe he thinks I'm particularly ugly. Maybe there's something on my face. That's why he's looking at me," Hugh said without looking at Sean.

He grabbed one of the boxes and turned to go back inside, but Sean planted his feet and stood in his path. He crossed his arms over his chest and stared at Hugh, to the point that it made Hugh uncomfortable. Sean could always see through Hugh, maybe because they were twins, or maybe because they'd grown up together. Hugh might be better at socializing with his brothers, but that didn't mean he wasn't uncomfortable, even with Sean. He didn't like the way Sean was looking at him, and he wasn't sure what to do.

"What's going on with you?" Sean asked.

"Nothing. I'm trying to do this so I can go home."

"And why are you in such a hurry to go home? I mean, I know you're used to staying in your apartment and never leaving, but we're helping Curtis, not a stranger. You don't have to be uncomfortable. You shouldn't be, not with us."

Hugh wanted to yell at Sean to leave him alone, but he knew better. He should give Sean what he wanted—a hint about what was going on with him. Sean would never leave him alone otherwise. "I never said I *wanted* to go home. I want this to be over. I don't know about you, but moving boxes isn't exactly my idea of having fun."

"No, your idea of having fun is being alone in your apartment." Sean reached out and grabbed the box Hugh was holding. He put it back into the van, and Hugh knew he wouldn't get out of this without talking to his brother.

He didn't want to, but he knew that if he didn't give Sean something, he would have to avoid him for the rest of the day. Maybe going home wasn't a bad idea after all. It would be rude, but as long as Hugh apologized to Manuel and Curtis, no one would probably care.

"I told you Leon is looking at you, and this is how you react?" Sean asked.

Hugh wanted to throttle him, and he pushed his hands into his pocket so he wouldn't be tempted. "How do you want me to react? Shall I spread him on the ground and have my wicked way with him?"

Sean blinked, then laughed. "That was specific. Have you been thinking about it?"

Hugh looked away. He was grateful that he wasn't a blusher, because he definitely would have been scarlet otherwise. So what if he'd been thinking about what he and Leon could get up to together? He knew it was a fantasy. He wasn't about to try anything, not in reality. "Why are you pushing? So what if he's looking at me? I told you, he probably thinks I look weird or something," he said instead of answering Sean's question.

Sean frowned. "You don't see that he's interested in you?"

"It looks to me that he's more interested in Jack and Andy." And it would make sense. Hugh wasn't sure how old Leon was, but he was ready to bet he was closer to Manuel's age than his. That meant that Jack and Andy, with their twenty-five and twenty-three years respectively, were closer to him in age. It was probably why they'd gravitated together. Well, that, and the fact that Leon seemed to flirt with everything that moved, and maybe a few things that didn't.

That didn't bother Hugh, except for the fact that Leon was ignoring him. He couldn't care less how easily Leon flirted with Jack and Andy, but he did wish Leon would flirt with him, too. Hell, he'd even flirted with Curtis, who was dating his best friend. He'd talked with Sean and had seemed to get along with him.

The only person Leon hadn't flirted with since they'd arrived was Hugh, and it hurt.

Hugh understood he wasn't everyone's cup of tea. Hell, at the moment, he was no one's cup of tea. He shouldn't be hurt. He was used to it. Even when he was with a group of friends—something that didn't often happen since he barely had friends in the first place—he was always the odd one out, the one who stayed silently hovering at the edge of the group and listening to what was happening without intervening. Maybe he shouldn't think about those people as friends but rather acquaintances. That felt closer to the truth. And today wasn't any different, even though Hugh was with his brothers. They were the ones who laughed and talked and had fun while he did most of the work in the background.

He turned and grabbed the box again. The sooner the van was empty, the sooner he could go home. He couldn't wait. "Just ignore it," he told Sean. "I told you. I'm fine, and Leon is probably looking at me because I remind him of his father or something. Let it go, yeah?"

Hugh headed toward the house without waiting for Sean to answer. He pushed the door open with his shoulder and stepped in, just in time to see Manuel poke his head into the entrance. Manuel smiled and held up his phone. "I'm ordering pizza. Are you okay with it?"

Hugh wasn't. He wanted to go home, but he didn't want to be rude. Manuel was in his life to stay, and they needed to be at the very least civil with each other. "Sure. I could eat."

Manuel beamed as if Hugh had made him the happiest man in the world. "Great. Why don't you put down that box and go wash your hands? The pizza will be here soon."

Hugh sighed. He wished this day was already over.

Leon's stomach growled. He patted it, smiling at Jack. "Can you tell I'm hungry?" he asked, teasing.

Jack chuckled. "I'm pretty sure all of us are. It's a small

miracle you're hungry, though, considering you haven't done anything today."

Leon narrowed his eyes at him. "How dare you? I directed the operations. It's only thanks to me that every box is in the room it belongs in."

Andy laughed. "True that. You might not have done any physical labor, but it doesn't mean you haven't done anything. Jack, stop being rude to him."

Leon couldn't help but smile. He hadn't been sure what to think of the brothers in the beginning, but they were good people. He got along with them pretty well, and he couldn't help but wonder if maybe they could be friends. He didn't want anything more than friendship with them, and he hoped that they were on board with that. They seemed to be for now, but that didn't mean much, from Leon's experience.

He knew they wouldn't be rude, though, whatever happened. They wouldn't want to create trouble, considering that Leon was Manuel's best friend and Curtis was their brother, but Leon wasn't sure what he wanted himself. He knew he needed friends. He couldn't just rely on Manuel for the rest of his life. Could he do this, though? Because he felt about friendship pretty much the same way that he felt about having a relationship. Eventually, people realized he wasn't worth it or that he was too complicated. Then they left, and he was alone again.

The only exception to that had been Manuel, and while he still wasn't leaving Leon behind, in a way, he was. He had Curtis now, and Leon knew that his and Manuel's friendship would change because of that. Manuel had been through a lot. He'd lost his mom, and he was still hurting over it. He deserved to be happy, and apparently, that happiness went through Curtis. That was okay with Leon, but he still wished things could go back to the way they'd been before. He realized it was selfish of him, though, which was why he'd given

Manuel and Curtis a wide berth today. Eventually, things would settle down, and they would find a new balance. In the meantime, though, Leon hated feeling like he wasn't sure what to do with his life.

"Why don't you grab glasses in the kitchen?" Manuel asked. "Pizza will be here in ten minutes."

Leon knew the house like the back of his hand, so he wasn't offended at the demand. Manuel was already working on emptying some of the boxes, even though they were full of Curtis' stuff. Leon would have felt awkward about touching stuff that wasn't his, but Manuel wasn't. Leon supposed that being in love meant this, too. You could look through your boyfriend's things without feeling weird about it.

"Are you giving me an order?" he asked, trying to keep things light.

Manuel rolled his eyes. "No, but apart from Curtis, who took the van back to his parents' house, you're the only one who knows where they are."

"Will he be back in time for dinner?"

"He should be. The house isn't that far away from here."

They could walk between the houses, which was how Manuel and Curtis had met. Leon wasn't sure he would be able to stand living so close to his in-laws, though. He loved his mom, yet he was more comfortable away from her. Manuel didn't seem to have a problem with it, which was great. He'd even spent Christmas with Curtis' family, and even though it had no doubt brought up memories of his mom, he seemed happy. Maybe this was what Curtis needed—a boyfriend with a big family who might not replace what he'd lost, but who could soothe over the wound and help it heal. Leon hadn't met Curtis' parents yet, and he wasn't planning to, but he liked that they'd welcomed and accepted Manuel into their life. Manuel had always been a family man. He deserved to have everything he'd ever wanted in life.

Leon headed to the kitchen, ignoring Jack and Andy, who were goofing around. The younger brother hadn't come, and neither had the one that came right after Curtis. Leon was a bit disappointed, but eventually, he would meet all of them. Seven brothers were a lot. He wasn't sure how Manuel would deal with all of those people, but it wasn't his business. He was Manuel's best friend, but he doubted he would be involved in that family's life.

He stepped into the kitchen and froze. He hadn't realized that Hugh was in here. Or was it Sean?

Leon eyed the man washing his hands at the sink and decided it was Hugh. He was pretty sure it was, anyway. There was something about him, a quiet strength, the feeling that even though he wasn't saying anything, his body was talking for him, that appealed to Leon. Sean didn't move the same way and didn't have that quiet strength about him, so Leon was pretty sure it wasn't him.

Well, whichever twin this was, it didn't change anything.

Leon headed to the cupboard with the glasses, and Hugh finally heard him and turned around. He seemed to freeze, too, and he grabbed the edge of the sink as if holding himself up. Leon smiled at him but focused on what he was doing.

He was flustered, though. He couldn't deny that, and he didn't know what to do about it. He wasn't even sure why he was feeling this way. Yes, Hugh was his type of man. He looked strong, and he was gorgeous. But more than that, it was his personality that appealed to Leon. He was quiet and gentle. Hugh would be so different from the men he slept with. Maybe *that* was why he was appealing, or perhaps it was just something else. Leon didn't know, and it didn't matter.

"Manuel sent me to grab glasses," he explained as he opened the cupboard. He glared at the glasses. The cabinets were just slightly too high for him, and he couldn't reach them without going on his tiptoes.

"He told me he was ordering pizza," Hugh said.

"He did. He said it should be here in about ten minutes. Hopefully, Curtis will be back by then. We wouldn't want him to eat cold pizza."

Hugh chuckled. "I don't think there'd be anything left for him to eat if he came back late. Jack and Andy can put away pizza like no one else."

Leon reached for one of the glasses and gently put it on the counter before taking a second one. "They did make it sound like they were starving."

"Well, they've been working today."

The third glass slipped from Leon's fingers, and Leon tried to grab it. A hand shot into his vision before he could, though, and Hugh's fingers wrapped around the glass before it could hit the counter and shatter.

Leon's heart was racing, and he tried to ignore it as he settled his feet to the floor and turned to Hugh. "Thank you."

Hugh was so close to him that Leon could smell him. He was wearing aftershave, or maybe cologne, and it smelled good, like a forest or something like that. It made Leon want to lean closer and take a better sniff, to lose himself in that scent. He was also close enough that he could feel Hugh's warmth through their clothes, and that meant that he was *too* close.

He smiled at Hugh and took a step back. "I would be grateful if you could grab the other glasses. I don't want to break anything."

Hugh was still staring at Leon, but Leon was grateful when he slowly nodded and did what Leon had asked. As soon as Leon had his glasses, he thanked Hugh and fled the kitchen. He had no idea what had just happened between them, and he didn't want to find out. It felt too dangerous, and Leon wasn't ready to put himself into that situation.

Not now, not yet, and maybe not ever.

CHAPTER THREE

Leon was Hugh's mate.

Hugh had a hard time believing it, but he couldn't deny what he'd smelled. He hadn't realized that earlier — he hadn't come close enough to Leon to smell him. He had now, though. He would have realized that Leon was his mate way sooner if he'd smelled him, but instead, he'd kept his distance, which probably had been a good thing. He didn't know how he would have reacted if he'd known sooner

He had no idea what to do about it. He wasn't even sure there *was* anything he could do about it.

He leaned back against the counter and stared at the door. Leon had already left, but Hugh could still smell him in the kitchen. It might be a trick of his brain or his nose, but he was almost a hundred percent sure that was the case. He was also almost a hundred percent sure that now that he'd smelled Leon, he would never be able to forget his scent. He would never be able to forget what had just happened, period.

He'd met his mate. He was the second brother of the seven of them to do so, and while his heart was racing, he wasn't sure whether or not to be happy about it.

He supposed that any of his other brothers except maybe Laurie and Andy would be over the moon. Sean definitely would. But Hugh was confused. He needed some time to wrap his mind around it, but he wasn't sure he'd have it, not with half of his brothers waiting for him in the other room.

Sure enough, Curtis' head popped through the kitchen doorway a few minutes later. He noticed Hugh standing there and stepped in, a frown forming on his face when he realized that Hugh wasn't doing anything. If he was honest with himself, Hugh wasn't sure there *was* anything he could do. He didn't feel able to do much more than breathe in and out and try to get over the shock.

"Hugh? Everything okay?" Curtis asked.

Hugh didn't know what to say, so he just shook his head. Then he nodded. Then he shook his head again.

Curtis' frown deepened, and he came to stand in front of Hugh. "You're scaring me. I don't understand if something happened or not. Can you tell me what's going on?"

Hugh opened his mouth and snapped it shut. What could he tell Curtis? Should he tell him about Leon being his mate? Curtis had told the entire family as soon as he'd met Manuel, and Manuel hadn't minded once he'd found out. Would Leon be okay with that? Or would he want Hugh to keep this to himself? Hugh didn't even know if Leon would ever consider being with him. Leon didn't know about shifters or mates, so he might freak out and run away. Even if he didn't, he might not appreciate people knowing that he and Hugh were linked this way, especially if he didn't want anything to do with Hugh.

"Do I need to call Mom?" Curtis said.

That was the ultimate threat. Hugh shook his head and opened his mouth, but only one word came out. "Leon."

Curtis blinked and looked at the kitchen door. "He was in here earlier, wasn't he? I think I saw him coming out with glasses."

Hugh nodded.

"And? What happened?" Curtis turned back to Hugh. "Did he say something to you? Did he *do* something to you? Did he hurt you?"

Curtis' voice was becoming louder, and Hugh needed him to shut up. "He didn't do anything," he finally managed to say.

"Are you sure? Because to me, it looks like something happened, and since the only word you managed to say was his name, I'm pretty sure he has something to do with whatever is happening to you." He turned toward the door, probably intending on snatching Leon to demand an explanation from him.

That would be the worst thing that could happen right now, so Hugh grabbed Curtis' arm. He couldn't allow his brother to run into the other room halfcocked and yell at Leon for something Leon wasn't even aware of.

"I promise he didn't do anything. I'm just in shock."

"You're in shock after he was in the kitchen. That means that something did happen." Curtis shook off Hugh's hand. "Dammit, Hugh. Either you tell me what happened, or I talk to Leon and demand an explanation from him. You don't have much of a choice. I'm not going to let anyone hurt my brother, not even my mate's best friend."

Hugh couldn't help but smile. "I'm the oldest here. I should be the one protecting you, not the other way around."

"That's bullshit. Apart from the fact that you're only three years older than me, it doesn't mean I can't protect you. That's what I'll do if I find out that someone is hurting you. Now talk."

Hugh hesitated. Part of him wanted to blurt out the truth. He wanted to tell Curtis what was going on and to have his support if he needed it, and he was pretty sure he would. But on the other hand, he didn't want Curtis to know, just in case Leon rejected him. What was Hugh going to do if that was what happened? Could he tell Curtis that Leon was his mate only to have to explain that Leon didn't want him?

It looked like he might not have a choice, though. Curtis looked ready to beat Leon into the ground, and Hugh couldn't allow that to happen.

He rubbed the back of his neck. "I promise you that Leon didn't do anything," he said, trying to find a way to put his thoughts into words without making a mess of it. He knew it wouldn't be enough, though. "I was washing my hands, and he came into the kitchen. He almost dropped a glass, but I managed to catch it before it hit the counter and chattered."

"That's not telling me anything."

"I had to step very close to him to help him. It was the only way for me to catch the glass." Hugh could still remember the warmth of Leon's body through their clothes and his scent invading his nose. He'd smelled sweet, but it wasn't anything Hugh could identify. Hugh wasn't sure whether or not he ever would be able to, but he could see himself trying for years to come.

"Hugh," Curtis said. He sounded irritated.

"When we were close, I smelled him. I never expected this to happen, but I realized he was my mate."

Curtis blinked and stared at Hugh. Hugh held his breath, wondering what was about to happen. He still wasn't sure what he thought about this. He wanted Curtis to be happy about it. He wanted himself to be happy about it, but he doubted he would be able to until he talked to Leon.

Right now, he had no way to know what Leon wanted. Leon didn't even know shifters existed. He probably thought they were a thing that only happened in movies and novels, but that wasn't the case. He could take it well or horribly, but Hugh hoped he would be like Manuel, who had taken it so well that he and Curtis had barely needed to talk about it. Hugh didn't doubt that Manuel had had questions, but from what Curtis had said, he'd accepted his swan side easily enough.

Would Leon? Or would he freak out? The same questions came back into Hugh's mind again and again, and Hugh didn't know what to do with them.

"Leon is your mate? You're sure about that?" Curtis asked quietly.

Hugh nodded. "I'm sure. I smelled him when he was close to me. He's my mate, Curtis."

Curtis slowly nodded and looked up at Hugh. "How do you feel about that?"

Hugh had no idea how to answer that question, but he had to. Curtis would worry otherwise, and there was no way to know what would happen then.

Leon was still wondering what had happened in the kitchen, but he was grateful he'd left Hugh behind. He kind of wanted to go back to ask Hugh what was going on, but he knew better than to do that, especially now that Curtis was in there with him.

He forced himself to smile at Manuel as he walked into the living room after washing his hands in the bathroom. He sat on the couch between Jack and Andy, reaching for the pizza box on the coffee table and snagging a slice. He also grabbed one of the napkins Manuel had put on the coffee table and bit into his pizza, but he didn't really taste it.

He couldn't stop thinking about Hugh.

Hugh wasn't the kind of guy Leon usually dated. *Dated* was the wrong word for what Leon did, though. He only had one-night stands, and he always had them with men who looked like him—short, thin, what people would think of as twinks. Leon understood them. They were simple to deal with, and since he always picked them up in clubs and bars, he knew they weren't after a relationship but just a bit of fun and pleasure, just the way Leon liked it.

Hugh, on the other hand, was obviously the kind of person who wanted something serious, and Leon couldn't give him or anyone else that.

"Move," Manuel said as he tried to fit his ass on the couch next to Leon.

Jack and Andy both glared at him. "Why should we move?" Jack asked.

"Because I want to sit next to my best friend. Come on. Move."

Leon was surprised at Manuel's words, but he probably shouldn't have been. He realized what was happening as soon as Manuel settled next to him, and he should have seen it coming.

"Okay. What's going on?" Manuel asked.

Of course Manuel had noticed something was up with Leon. Sometimes, Leon wished Manuel didn't know him as well as he did, but there was no changing that. Leon wasn't giving up on their friendship for anything, not even a conversation he wished he could avoid.

"I'm fine." But he'd been spending much more time with his boyfriend, and that meant less time with Leon. Leon felt slightly jealous and envious. It was normal, though, and that was okay. But maybe it was time for Leon to find himself another friend, or at least an acquaintance that wasn't his mother. That meant letting someone in, though, and he wasn't sure he could do that.

He didn't want Manuel to know he was interested in Hugh. He shouldn't be, and only bad things could come out of anyone else knowing what was going on. He trusted Manuel, of course, but he couldn't risk it.

What if Manuel said something in front of Hugh? What if somehow, Hugh found out that Leon was interested in him? Leon couldn't imagine Hugh would be interested. He was such a serious man, and gentle and sweet, too. He was the kind of man who deserved much more than Leon, and Leon didn't want to stand in the way. He wanted Hugh to have everything he deserved and wanted. Sticking around might stop that from happening.

"I told you I'm fine," he told Manuel in a last, desperate attempt to get his best friend to leave him alone.

"And I told you I don't believe you. What happened in the kitchen? I saw you come out of it in a rush, and Curtis has been in there for ten minutes with Hugh."

"Hugh found me," Leon admitted. "Or rather, I found him. He was in the kitchen when I went there."

Manuel's eyes widened, and he bounced once. "So? What did he say?"

Leon narrowed his eyes. Had Manuel sent him into the kitchen on purpose? He wouldn't put it past him. Now that Manuel was blissfully happy, he wanted everyone to feel the same, but especially Leon. "Nothing. What was he supposed to say? He was washing his hands. I grabbed the glasses and got out of the kitchen. That's all."

Manuel didn't look convinced. This was once again a sign that he knew Leon better than Leon knew himself sometimes. It was annoying, but it was also a relief sometimes.

Now wasn't one of those times.

"You can talk to me if you need to," Manuel murmured.

"I know."

"Even if it involves Curtis' brothers. Curtis might be my mate—man, but that doesn't mean I'll always be on his side, not if I'm not okay with it. If Hugh said anything bad to you, I'll kick his ass."

Leon couldn't help but laugh at that image. "You'll kick his ass? He's what, one foot taller than you are?"

Manuel gently slapped Leon's thigh. "Not a whole foot."

"Something close, though."

"He's not that tall."

"Okay, so he's not. Still. You're not a fighter, Manu. We both know that. And he *is* taller and broader than you."

Manuel shrugged, but he looked embarrassed. "I can learn

to fight if it means keeping you safe and happy."

Leon was touched, but he didn't need this. "Thank you. I don't have anything to talk to you about, though. I promise. Like I told you, I grabbed the glasses and came back."

"I want you to be part of my life, and since Curtis is, too, his brothers will be. I want you to be comfortable with all of them. I know they're a lot and that you're a loner, but do you think you can do that?"

Leon finally realized what was happening. Manuel was worried about him, but he was also worried about himself. Having Curtis move in with him was a huge step, especially considering they hadn't known each other for more than a few months. Manuel was no doubt nervous about that and worrying about possibly losing Leon didn't help. Add to that Curtis' huge family, and it could be the recipe for a disaster if Manuel wasn't careful.

"He loves you," Leon quietly said. "And while it's true that meeting his entire family isn't your idea of fun, I'm positive you can become part of them. It's obvious that they love you as much as Curtis does." Leon had watched the brothers and how they acted with Manuel, and he was sure of that. If Curtis' parents loved Manuel half as much as his brothers did, Manuel would be set for life. He would finally have the family he'd always wanted and the one he deserved. He'd thought he'd lost that possibility when his mother had died, but now, he had it again.

Leon looked at the kitchen door. Curtis was still in there, and so was Hugh. Had something happened? Should Leon check?

"They're probably talking," Manuel said because he'd noticed Leon watching the kitchen door.

"How do you know?"

"They like to talk, especially if I'm not around."

Leon frowned. "And that doesn't bother you?"

"Why should it?"

"Well, it's taking a lot of time away from Curtis and you."

Manuel chuckled and shook his head. "Don't you see? I have all the time in the world with Curtis. I already know his family is going to be a part of it, and that's fine with me. There might be a lot of them, but they're good people, and they accepted me when I wasn't even sure I wanted to be with Curtis. Besides, I've always known Curtis was close to them. That's not going to change, even though he's with me now, and I don't expect it to."

Leon had never known anything like that. He had his mother, of course, and he'd had his father for the first part of his life, but that didn't mean he was comfortable thinking about family. He wouldn't even know what to do if he had one.

No. He was much better by himself, with just Manuel and his mother, and maybe a few more people. He couldn't make himself vulnerable to a lot of people. He wouldn't be able to stand it if he was told that he was an abomination and a crime against nature one more time. He'd already gone through it once, and that had been enough.

He wouldn't put himself through that again, not even potentially. That was one thing he was sure of. He was never letting his father's—or anyone else's—words hurt him again.

"I don't know. I'm happy?" Hugh sounded hesitant to his own ears, though. He didn't know how he felt apart from confused and frightened.

"That's great," Curtis said.

Hugh snorted. He wasn't sure it was. "He's probably not interested," he said.

Curtis frowned. "Why are you saying that?"

Hugh snorted and gestured at himself. "Have you seen

me? And have you seen *him*? Why would he be interested? He can have anyone he wants, so why would he want me?"

"That's bullshit. Come on, Hugh. Stop that. I don't see what the problem is. It's not like you're a monster or anything. You're a good guy and decent-looking, and maybe I'm biased because I'm your brother, but I think you and Leon would fit well together."

Hugh kept his mouth shut. He knew Curtis meant well, but also that he didn't understand. No one did, except maybe Sean, but even he would push Hugh to talk to Leon and find a way they could be together.

And if Hugh was honest with himself, that was what he wanted. He wanted to be with Leon. He'd wanted Leon even before he realized they were mates, but now, he had a hard time ignoring those feelings. He had to, though. He didn't want to freak Leon out, and he didn't want to hope. It would be too crushing to be rejected after that.

"Let's go eat, okay?" Curtis asked. "You don't have to do anything about this now. Did you say anything to him about it?"

"Of course not." Even if he'd planned to, he couldn't have, because Leon had run away as soon as he'd seemed to realize something was happening. He hadn't even looked back, which in Hugh's opinion was yet another reason not to get his hopes up. "He doesn't know shifters are real, does he?"

"As far as I know, he doesn't, but I'll ask Manuel. Maybe he told him. I wouldn't be surprised if that were the case. But let's have some pizza before Jack and Andy eat all of it. You can take your time to think about it and decide what you want to do."

"All right." Curtis wasn't wrong. Hiding in the kitchen wouldn't help, and Hugh was hungry. Maybe once dinner was over, he could go home and think about this and come up with a plan. He wasn't so sure one existed, but what else was he supposed to do?

He followed Curtis back into the living room, where everyone was sitting on the couch. It was a tight fit, and Manuel had dragged a few chairs from the kitchen so everyone would have a place to sit. Hugh wasn't surprised to see that Leon was on the couch with Andy. He ignored them and sat into one of the chairs, taking a slice of pizza and staring straight ahead.

He was always awkward, but today was even worse. He wanted to look at Leon. He wanted to find out if Leon was looking at him or if Sean had been lying earlier when he'd said that. He also didn't want to find out, though. He was a mess of emotions, and he didn't know how to try to untangle them. Was it even possible?

Luckily for him, no one said anything about how silent he was during the meal. His family was used to it. He'd always been the silent one, especially next to his younger brothers, who were always bouncing off the walls. Jack and Andy joked around, talked, and Leon was right there with them, laughing at whatever they said. He wasn't quite flirting with them anymore, but it was obvious they would become friends eventually, and Hugh didn't know how to feel about that.

He wanted his mate to get along with his brothers, but he didn't even know if he and Leon would get together. What if Leon became friends with one of Hugh's brothers and Hugh had to see him every day even though they weren't together? What if Hugh told Leon about all of this, and Leon rejected him? What if Leon fell in love with one of Hugh's brothers? It was a possibility. Hugh didn't want to think about it, but maybe he should.

Or maybe he should stop thinking about this tonight. He wouldn't solve anything, especially since he still had to talk to Leon. He needed to focus on something else, but he was having a hard time. Every time he thought he'd managed,

Leon did something that made Hugh look at him. He was good-spirited, and it was obvious he was having fun. Hugh, on the other hand, felt frozen. He was separated from the group, and that was his fault. He didn't mind, though. He never wanted to be in the spotlight, but especially so now.

Once everyone was done eating, they helped Manuel and Curtis clean up. It was weird to think that Curtis lived here now, but Hugh was happy for his brother. It had to feel good to finally be able to move out of their parents' house, especially after living away from them for years before coming back.

"Leon needs a ride home," Manuel said.

Hugh blinked. "Does he?"

"We can drive him," Andy volunteered.

Hugh wasn't surprised. He nodded at them and headed to the door, but of course, Curtis had something to say about it. "It would be easier if Hugh did it," he said. "You can take Sean home, though."

Jack frowned. "Why?"

"Because Leon's house is on the way to Hugh's, but Sean's isn't. It would be faster and easier for everyone if you took Sean home while he took Leon."

Leon glared playfully. "What are you doing? Fighting over who's taking me home?"

Hugh shook his head and narrowed his eyes at his brother. Curtis wasn't looking at him, but he knew what he was doing. Hugh was sure of that. He was trying to give Leon and Hugh some time alone, but Hugh already knew it wouldn't work. He didn't have the balls to talk to his mate. He wouldn't be able to tell Leon anything about this.

No matter how many times the words moved to his lips, he couldn't push them out. Maybe it was because other people surrounded him and Leon, but Hugh knew himself. He always felt more comfortable not talking about things. It was easier to ignore them than to put everything out there and fight or talk things out. He doubted that anything would change even if he and Leon ended up in a car alone together. Hell, they would probably become even more uncomfortable than they already were, and that wasn't something Hugh wanted to deal with right now.

It looked like he might have to, though.

Manuel's expression lit up. "That's a great idea. And you're right. Leon's apartment is closer to Hugh's."

"It's not a problem for us," Jack insisted.

Hugh couldn't help but wonder if Jack was interested in Leon. He wouldn't be surprised if he was. Leon lit up the room, and everyone seemed to be attracted to his light. Hugh hoped he wouldn't have to watch Jack and Leon date. If that happened, he wouldn't tell Leon they were mates, but that was the only thing he was sure of right now. He needed a few hours on his own to think things through and make decisions, and that meant he needed to go home as soon as possible.

"Let Hugh do this," Curtis said, glaring at Jack and trying to tell him something with his gaze.

Jack was ignoring him because he wasn't saying something Jack wanted, though.

"You guys don't have to fight over me. I can call a cab," Leon said. He looked worried, which Hugh hated. He didn't want his mate to feel awkward and pulled on by several different people. Leon should do what Leon wanted, whatever that was.

"You don't need to get a cab. We have enough cars between us to drive you home," Curtis insisted.

Leon could tell Hugh wasn't enthusiastic about giving a ride home, though. He didn't want to offend Curtis, who seemed convinced that it was the best idea ever, so he didn't know what to do. "Since you're fighting over me, maybe I *should* get a cab," he said.

Curtis shook his head. "You shouldn't have to pay for something we can give you for free. Come on. Hugh is more than happy to drive you home."

He said so while glaring at Jack, and Leon was aware of the fact that something was happening that he couldn't read. The brothers were silently communicating with each other, and none of them looked happy. He wasn't about to touch that with a ten-foot pole, so he slowly nodded and turned to look at Hugh. "Are you sure?"

He needed to be. Leon couldn't say he was looking forward to spending any length of time alone with Hugh. He hoped he wasn't going to say or do something he would regret eventually. He found Hugh attractive, and for whatever reason, he wanted to spend time with him, even though he knew it was the worst idea ever.

No matter how perfect Hugh seemed, Leon couldn't get close to him. It didn't matter that he wanted to. He didn't date. He didn't have boyfriends. He didn't allow people to get close to him. It was a small miracle that Manuel had managed, but that was where things ended. Leon wasn't looking for a boyfriend, especially not one who was related to his best friend. He didn't want to make a mess and ruin everything for Manuel, which meant that all of Curtis' brothers were off the table, even Jack, who was looking at him like he was trying to read him and who seemed to be flirting with him especially hard. Leon shouldn't have gone along with it, but it was too late.

Hugh nodded curtly. "I can give you a ride home. It's not a problem."

It looked like it might be. It also looked like Hugh wasn't happy about it. But he'd said yes, and it felt safer than going with Jack.

Leon forced himself to smile at Jack. "See? Not a problem. But thanks for offering. I'll see you soon?"

Jack nodded and started talking about exchanging numbers, but Leon had already checked out. He was keeping an eye on Hugh and wondering what was going to happen.

Things had been awkward between him and Hugh, especially in the kitchen. Leon still wasn't sure what had happened, but he did know *something* had. Maybe he'd find out, or perhaps he and Hugh would stay silent and awkward the entire ride home.

That was what happened. After they'd said their goodbyes, they headed to Hugh's car. Leon wasn't known for being silent, but for whatever reason, he couldn't seem to find a topic to talk about. Nothing felt safe, not with Hugh, and with Hugh's scent wrapping around him, making him feel like he was home, it was even harder. Leon didn't understand why he was feeling this way, and he couldn't wait to get out of the car.

The silence between him and Hugh was tense, and Leon tapped his fingertips on his thigh as he looked outside the window. He wanted to say something and break the awkwardness. He and Hugh were in each other's lives to stay. Curtis and Manuel seemed to be in their relationship for the long-run, and while Leon was happy for them, it also meant that he had to deal with all of Curtis' brothers, including Hugh.

"So, you haven't told me what you do," he said, trying to start a conversation.

Hugh grunted and kept his gaze on the road. "I work from home."

That didn't give Leon a lot to work with. "Really? And what you do from home? I work from home, too, although I'm pretty sure you're not a writer like I am."

Hugh gave him a sideways glance. "You're right. I'm not a

writer."

That was it. It was all Hugh said, and again, Leon was a bit lost. He usually had easy conversations with pretty much everyone, but Hugh was making it hard. Or maybe it was whatever energy crackled between them. Leon didn't know, and he didn't think it mattered.

Even though he would have to deal with having Hugh in his life, it wasn't like they would see each other often. Hell, it would probably be months before they spent time together again. He could avoid going to Manuel and Curtis' house if he knew Hugh was there. It would be fairly easy, at least until Manuel caught on. But in the meantime, Leon would be able to avoid Hugh, and that felt like a good thing right now.

He'd never been so grateful when Hugh finally parked in front of his apartment building. He reached for the door, ready to bolt, but Hugh's voice stopped him. "I'm sorry," Hugh said.

Leon bit his lower lip. He wanted to run, but he also wanted to find out what Hugh was sorry for. He had to make a decision, and when he did, he let go of the door and slowly turned to face Hugh. "What are you sorry about?"

Hugh shrugged without looking at Leon. "I know I'm not the friendliest person. You've been trying to make conversation, and I haven't made it easy on you. I apologize."

"It's fine. I know not everyone is as friendly as me, or that not everyone wants to talk to me. I'm not offended."

"But I do want to talk to you. I'd like to see you again."

It took a second for Leon to understand what he was saying, and even then, he had to make sure. "You want to see me again?"

Hugh scowled, and it shouldn't have been as adorable as it was. "That's what I said, isn't it?"

"Well, yes, but you've been avoiding me for most of the day. Why would you want to see me again?"

"Because you're cute. You're sweet. You're a good friend, and you're a lot of fun."

Leon hadn't realized that Hugh had been watching him, but he had to have been. Instead of telling him how beautiful he was and how good they would be together, he'd said Leon was cute. Then he'd added a lot of other stuff that people didn't usually notice. Leon was touched, and it was confusing. He'd just been telling himself that he needed to stay away from Hugh, yet now, he felt the urge to say yes.

He wanted to date Hugh.

He wanted to do it, but he already knew it wouldn't end well. He shook his head. "I don't date."

Hugh jerked back as if Leon had hit him. "Of course. I should have realized. I'm sorry. Please ignore everything I just said. Have a good evening."

The transformation was instant. Hugh had been nervous and awkward before, but now, he was downright cold, and his back was ramrod straight. He was pushing Leon away before Leon could hurt him even more than he already had, and Leon felt guilty. He knew he shouldn't. He didn't date, but it was an especially bad idea considering who Hugh was.

Leon cleared his throat. "You don't understand. It has nothing to do with you. I don't date anyone, ever."

"Why?"

That was the hundred-dollar question, wasn't it? "I don't want to talk about it. I'm sorry if I led you on. I should have been clearer."

"You did nothing wrong. I expected that answer anyway."

There was something in the way Hugh said it that told Leon he was used to rejection, or maybe that he'd been shielding himself for one. Leon didn't like it, but there was nothing he could do about it.

He swallowed. "As I was saying, it doesn't have anything to do with you. I would have said no to your brother, too, if he'd given me a ride home instead of you. I don't date, and that's it. It doesn't matter how nice or how sexy you are, my answer is still no. I'm sorry."

"Don't be sorry. It's your prerogative to say no to anyone you want to say no to. *I* am sorry."

Leon huffed out a laugh. "We've been apologizing to each other for the last few minutes, and it hasn't solved anything." He reached for the door again. "I should go. But I want you to know that it doesn't have anything to do with you. Dating is something I have a problem with, and I'm sure that any other man would be more than happy to be with you." Just not Leon.

But that was a lie, wasn't it? Leon would be more than happy to date Hugh. He just couldn't, not now, and probably not ever.

CHAPTER FOUR

I *don't date.*

Hugh couldn't forget Leon's words. He'd said them before leaving the car and running away as if he expected Hugh to go after him, but Hugh had just watched him from the car until he was inside his apartment building. Once Leon was inside, Hugh had waited some more, until he was as sure as he could that Leon was safely home. Then he'd driven away, and he hadn't seen Leon since then.

He also hadn't been able to stop thinking about him.

Hugh had tried going back to his life, but it wasn't easy. He'd been with Leon for only a few hours, yet Leon was everywhere. Hugh thought about him when he was having breakfast in the morning and when he was grocery shopping. He thought about Leon when he watched TV at night and when he went to bed. He thought about Leon as soon as he opened his eyes in the morning, and Leon was the last thought he had at night.

In short, Hugh was going crazy, and he didn't know what to do about it.

He'd also been ignoring his brothers. He knew he shouldn't, because they wouldn't let him do it for much longer, but he wasn't up to talking to any of them, not even Sean, and *especially* Jack and Curtis. Jack, because Leon had been flirting with him, and even though Hugh didn't think anything had happened between them, he couldn't help but feel jealous. Curtis, because he knew that Leon was Hugh's mate and he would no doubt start pushing for Hugh to do something about it.

Hugh still didn't know what to do. He wanted to talk to Leon, of course, but he doubted Leon would listen, and he didn't want to be stalkerish. Leon wanted space, and he clearly didn't want anything to do with Hugh, so Hugh would stay away.

He had to.

He turned his attention back to his computer screen, even though he knew it would be a moot point. He'd barely been able to work since he'd met Leon, but he had to at least try, and he managed, for a handful of minutes.

Then someone knocked on the door. Hugh ignored it. He hoped it was the postman or someone like that so he wouldn't have to talk to them, and he grimaced when he heard the sound of a key sliding into the keyhole. Since whoever was there was coming in, it had to be either his parents or one of his brothers. He was ready to bet it was Sean. He often behaved as if Hugh's place was an extension of his apartment. He didn't have problems walking in, especially when he was angry at Hugh or worried.

Hugh was ready to bet Sean was worried right now. He understood why. If Sean had been acting like he was, he would be worried, too. Sean couldn't understand what was happening because Hugh hadn't told him. He hadn't told anyone but Curtis, and he'd already regretted that.

"Hugh?" Sean called out.

Hugh stayed silent and fake-worked. He knew he wouldn't be able to focus with Sean in the apartment, though. Besides, he suspected Sean would start yelling at him as soon as he found him, so he saved everything that needed to be saved and turned his chair around just as Sean stepped into the office.

Sean froze and glared at Hugh. "What the fuck? Couldn't you answer? I thought I was going to find you dead or something."

Hugh shrugged. "I'm not dead, as you can see. I'm fine, actually, so you can go." Hugh knew it wouldn't work, but he could still hope.

Sean crossed his arms over his chest. "I'm not going anywhere. I want to know what's wrong."

Hugh didn't want to tell him. "Nothing is wrong."

"Bullshit. It's seven PM, and you're still wearing pajamas."

Hugh looked down at himself. It was true. "It's because I'm more comfortable. I work from home, remember? I can wear pajamas all day if I want to."

"But I know you don't. Even though you work from home, you like to get dressed in the morning. This is not like you. What also isn't like you is that you haven't been answering my texts, and you haven't been talking to any of us. Even Mom is starting to get worried, and she only didn't come because I told her I would talk to you."

Hugh winced. "I'm freaking thirty-five years old. Is it too much to ask the bunch of you to leave me alone?"

Sean's expression shifted. He was still angry, but he looked even more worried than he had before.

Hugh knew he'd said the wrong thing.

"What's going on?" Sean asked again. "And don't tell me it's nothing, because I don't believe you. You just said you didn't want us to stick our noses into your business, and you would never have said that if something wasn't happening."

Hugh rubbed his face with both his hands. He was tired, mostly because he couldn't sleep. Every time he closed his eyes, he saw Leon. He was starting to get worried about how obsessed he seemed to be with his mate, and he wondered if it was because of his swan half. He knew his swan wanted to go to Leon and convince him to be with them, but Hugh didn't know how to do that.

"I'm fine," he said with a sigh. "I promise. I'm just busy,

and I don't want you to worry about me."

"But don't you see? Of course we worry about you. We love you. We want to make sure you're okay, and to me, you don't look okay. Not only are you still wearing your pajamas, but you look like you haven't shaved in several days."

That was because Hugh hadn't. He hadn't shaved since he'd met Leon.

Dammit. Would he ever be able to stop thinking about his mate? He wanted to, so badly that he was ready to do just about anything to make that happen, but he knew it would be nearly impossible. Maybe if he talked to Leon and explained what was happening and Leon rejected him, he could put this to rest. He wasn't a hundred percent sure that would work, though, and even though he wanted to be brave, Hugh still feared the rejection.

Sean came closer and crouched next to Hugh's chair. He put a hand on Hugh's knee and squeezed. "Look, it's obvious something is going on with you, even though you don't want to talk about it. And that's fine. I want to know because I want to help you solve whatever problem you have, but if you don't want to tell me, then I'll back off. But I need to know you're okay. We all do."

"Leon is my mate," Hugh blurted out. He hadn't meant to say it, but now that the words were out, he felt better. Only slightly, but better.

Sean blinked. "Leon? You mean Manuel's best friend?"

Hugh glared at him. "Do you know many Leons?"

"Well, no, but I wanted to be sure. So he's your mate? *That's* your problem? Is that why you haven't been leaving your house?"

"Mostly."

"Why? Did he push you away? Did he reject you?"

Hugh shook his head. "He doesn't even know shifters exist."

Sean leaned back and looked up at Hugh. "Let me guess. You haven't talked to him at all, have you?"

"I haven't," Hugh confirmed

"Why?

"When I drove him home, I told him I wanted to see him again, and he said he didn't date. He said it wasn't anything to do with me. He doesn't date anyone." Hugh snorted softly. "I doubt that's the truth, but I didn't push."

"But maybe if you told him everything, he would understand. I mean, he's your mate. He might not want to date right now, but at least tell him that shifters are a thing and that he's your mate."

Hugh shook his head. "I can't tell him he's my mate. I don't want him to think that he *has* to be with me even though he doesn't want to."

"So, what—you're just going to give up?"

"Of course not."

"Are you sure? Because to me, it looks like that's what you did."

He wasn't wrong. Hugh hadn't even tried to contact Leon. He didn't have Leon's phone number, but it would be fairly easy to get it. He only had to call Manuel, or even Curtis. He hadn't, though. He wasn't planning to. He didn't want Leon to think they had to be together when Leon didn't want a relationship, not even with Hugh, or maybe especially not with him. Leon had been clear—he didn't date. He didn't do boyfriends.

In a sense, it made Hugh feel better. He wasn't sure he could stand seeing Leon day in and day out, maybe being friends with him, and not being able to touch him or kiss him. It probably made him an asshole, but he couldn't help how he felt.

But at least he wouldn't have to watch Leon with someone else.

He was half in love with Leon already, and he barely knew him. It would be too easy to lose himself in the feelings he had for his mate, and he couldn't allow that to happen, not when Leon didn't want it. *No.* Hugh was better off staying away from Leon.

He just had to convince Sean of that. Probably the rest of his family, too. He wasn't looking forward to it at all. They were all stubborn, so it would be a case of who could out stubborn the others.

The music made everything pound around Leon, and he tried to focus on the rhythm, moving his body along. The problem was that he couldn't stop thinking about Hugh.

He sighed. He should have known better than to come out tonight. He hadn't been able to stop thinking about Hugh. No matter how many times he told himself he needed to stop, Hugh was always at the center of his thoughts, even in the middle of the club with a bunch of people dancing around and almost on top of Leon.

What was Leon supposed to do? He'd thought that coming to the club and maybe finding someone would help push thoughts of Hugh away, but so far, no one had caught his eye. He wasn't usually this picky, and he probably should stop and grab the first twink he found and drag him to the bathroom.

Yes. That was what he should do. The problem was that he couldn't forget Hugh's disappointed expression when Leon had told him he didn't date. He hadn't heard from him since then, although he wasn't sure why he'd expected to. It wasn't like he and Hugh were friends, or like Hugh had his phone number. Besides, one rejection was probably enough.

But had it really been a rejection? Leon couldn't believe Hugh really wanted to date him. It was probably wishful thinking. Maybe Hugh had just been trying to be nice. He was a stable kind of man, someone who would make another guy happy.

But not Leon. Never Leon.

Hugh deserved better. He deserved better than the broken heart Leon still carried around after what his father had done. He deserved better than Leon, who was hiding behind his shield of makeup and weird clothes.

Leon could have kissed the guy dancing next to him when his phone vibrated in his pocket, saving him from his thoughts. He'd come to the club to distract himself, but so far, it hadn't worked, and he hoped whoever was calling would help with that. He pushed away from the crowd, headed outside, his phone already in his hand. He answered as soon as the door was closing behind him. "Manu!"

He stepped away from the people smoking by the door so he would have a bit of privacy and wouldn't stink of cigarettes once he was done.

"Where are you?" Manuel asked.

"At the club."

"Really?"

"Of course. Why would I be lying?"

"I don't know. I thought you and Hugh hit it off. Or maybe it was you and Jack?"

"I don't see what it has to do with me being at the club."

"Well, you're there when you want to pick up a guy. I thought that maybe you'd pick up Hugh."

Shit. "That's never going to happen."

"Why not?"

"Because I don't date, remember? And Curtis' brothers deserve better than that. They're probably after a relationship." Especially Hugh. It was just a guess, but Leon suspected that was the case even though he didn't know him well.

"I still don't get why you don't want a relationship."

"I'm not a romantic like you. I don't believe there's one man for me out there. Since I don't, it's better for me to try all the guys I can get my hands on, isn't it?"

"If you say so." But Manuel didn't sound convinced, and Leon didn't blame him. "I don't know about that. To me, it sounds like maybe you want to talk. Why haven't you called me?"

Leon had expected that, but he wasn't sure how to answer. "Why should I have called you? You have stuff to do. You're settling in with Curtis. You're still in the honeymoon phase of your relationship. I know he won't ask you to dump me as a friend, but that doesn't mean he wants to listen to you talking to me. Come on, Manuel. You just moved in together. Why aren't you guys fucking all over the place?"

Manuel made a spluttering noise.

Leon laughed. He knew his friend was blushing. That was why he'd said what he'd said.

"What are you talking about?" Manuel cried out.

"You two just moved in together. Shouldn't you be christening all the rooms?"

"I'm worried about you, and Curtis is worried about Hugh."

Leon didn't like the sound of that. "Why? Has something happened?"

"He's not answering phone calls or texts. Curtis says that while he's usually pretty isolated, that's not like him. It's almost like he's changed since he's met you."

Leon bristled. "Are you implying that I had something to do with it?"

"Maybe. I'm not saying you did it on purpose or anything, but it sounds to me like he didn't take your rejection well."

"And what do you want me to do with that?"

"I don't know. I want both you and Hugh to be happy, and I wish I could do something to make it happen."

Leon smiled, even though Manuel couldn't see him. "Well, you don't have to worry about me. I *am* happy."

"Are you sure that's the case, though? Or are you just lying to yourself and to me?"

That was way too close for comfort. Leon pushed away from the wall and headed back toward the door. "Do you have anything else to tell me? Or can I go back inside and find someone to fuck in the bathroom?"

Manuel *tsked*. "The bathroom? You don't even bring them back to your apartment?"

"As if. What if the guy is a serial killer or something? Then you'll find my body cut into pieces in plastic bags, and all because I wanted to get laid. Nope, I'm not risking it. All the sex I have will be in the bathroom, or if it's occupied, out here in the alley." Although Leon wasn't looking forward to that—from experience, he knew it was cold and that people stumbled onto you more often than not.

"I don't know how you do it."

"That's because you're monogamous by nature. I'm not. Now go back to your boyfriend. Climb him like a tree or something. I'm going to find someone of my own to fuck."

"Fine. But if you need anything, call me. I'll always answer."

"I know, sweetheart. See you tomorrow?"

"Of course. You know where to find me."

Leon hung up and looked at the door. He straightened his back and tilted his chin up.

He could forget Hugh. He was going to do everything he could to make that happen, and that meant getting laid.

He strode back inside the bar, excited at the thought of finding someone who could fuck the thoughts of Hugh away.

Sean had been weirdly quiet after yelling at Hugh, and Hugh

knew he was planning something. He'd been on his phone most of the time since he'd arrived at the apartment, texting, making Hugh wonder who he was talking to and what he was plotting. *Because he's planning something*. There was no doubt about that.

Hugh did his best to ignore his brother, trying to focus on the computer screen instead. He was getting hungry, though, but he wasn't about to show that to Sean. Sean had asked him a few times to stop working since it was already so late, but stopping would mean Hugh would have to focus on his brother, and that wasn't something he wanted to do.

He couldn't believe that he'd blurted out the truth. Sean had been stunned, then rude when he'd said that he couldn't believe Hugh was giving up so easily.

Hugh *wasn't* giving up. There wasn't anything to give up. Leon had been clear that he didn't want to date, and Hugh didn't want to push him. Did that make him a quitter? Maybe, but he liked to believe that it also made him a good mate. If Leon didn't want him, he wasn't going to force him. He respected Leon's needs.

Sean suddenly rose from the couch at the back of the room Hugh used as this office. "Right. You need to change. We're going out."

Hugh sighed. He knew something like that was coming. "I'm not going anywhere. I'm still working."

"You better save whatever you're working on, because I'm turning off your computer."

He would do it, too, so Hugh rushed into saving everything as Sean slowly came closer. He even turned his computer off, just in case, then turned to glare at his brother. "What do you want from me? I don't want to go out. I'm fine here."

"Well, you don't look fine. Besides, I want to have some fun with my brother. You can either change, or I can drag you out in your pajamas. Your choice." Sean looked Hugh up and down. "I mean, your pajamas are cute, but they're pajamas. It might give people the wrong idea."

Hugh hesitated. He didn't want to go out. He didn't want to do anything but work and sleep. But he knew Sean, and he knew how stubborn his twin brother was. If he didn't agree to this, Sean *would* drag him out in his pajama pants, and that was probably not the best idea. Hugh also couldn't keep Sean out. Not only would Sean kick up a fuss, but he would no doubt also tell their mom, and then, Hugh would be in trouble. Sean had mentioned something about her already being worried, and this would make it worse. It was the last thing Hugh needed, so he reluctantly got to his feet, still glaring at Sean.

"Fine. I'm going to get dressed. Where are we going?"

Sean grinned. "I thought a club? Wear something nice, will you?"

Hugh groaned. "I don't want to go dancing. I hate clubs even when I'm feeling good. What makes you think I'm going to enjoy myself tonight?"

"Don't know, and honestly, I don't care. Go get dressed. You have ten minutes."

Hugh was ready in five. He didn't like clubs or dancing or making a fool of himself in public in general, so he didn't make much of an effort, throwing on jeans and a button-down shirt and quickly finger-combing his hair. He considered shaving, but he couldn't find the energy to do it. He wasn't looking forward to going to the club, but hopefully, he would be able to stand in the background while Sean had fun. Even though he was going with Sean, there was no way Sean would be able to force him to dance.

Right?

Sean was bouncing his knee and was still on his phone when Hugh went back. He looked up, stared at Hugh for a moment, then shrugged. "I guess you'll do."

Hugh looked down at himself. "What's wrong with what I'm wearing?"

"Well, it's not very seductive."

"That's because I'm not planning on seducing anyone. I'm only going out because you'll threaten me if I don't. I'm not planning on picking up anyone." And not only because those people wouldn't be Leon.

Hugh suspected it would take him a while to get over the loyalty he felt for Leon. They were mates, so it was inevitable that both he and his swan wanted Leon. They viewed him as the only man they could be with, since he was their mate, and Hugh wasn't sure he *could* get over it. That meant Hugh wasn't about to try to seduce anyone else.

He and Sean left the apartment, and Hugh made sure to grumble the entire way. He wanted Sean to know what he thought of what they were doing, although he suspected his brother already did. Sean was good at ignoring him, though, and he focused on the road until they got to a club. Hugh had no idea which one—he wasn't a club guy, and he wasn't planning on changing that anytime soon.

Sean found a spot in the parking lot and turned to face Hugh. "Okay. Leon is in there."

Hugh blinked. "Leon?"

"Yes. I asked Manuel to ask him where he was, and this was the answer."

"For fuck's sake, Sean. Why are you doing this? I don't want to see Leon, and he doesn't want to see me."

"Correction—you desperately want to see him, and we don't know what he wants. He might have told you he doesn't date, but that doesn't mean it's the entire truth, and it's not fair that he doesn't know what's between the two of you. You need to tell him before making any kind of decision. He deserves to know. He's your mate, not just a guy you like."

"And you thought that coming here was a good idea? What

do you expect me to do? Find him, go up to him, and tell him *hey, I'm a swan shifter, and you're my mate, which means that we're perfect for each other and destined to be together.*"

Sean rubbed his chin. "That's actually not a bad idea. It certainly takes care of everything you need to tell him."

Hugh huffed and opened the car door, sliding out and slamming it shut. He looked at the club. He could feel the music vibrating already, and he wasn't even anywhere near close to the entrance. He didn't want to go inside.

He didn't like clubs. He didn't like dancing. He didn't like crowds and having people look at him and judge him. He knew he wasn't going anywhere, though. Sean wanted him to do this, and Hugh was going to have to follow his lead.

He hated that idea. He didn't want to push Leon into anything Leon didn't want, but that was exactly what would happen if Sean had his way. But maybe they wouldn't find Leon. Maybe he'd already left.

Hugh gently snorted. "You're a dick," he told Sean. Because of course, Leon would be inside. That was just Hugh's luck.

Sean clapped Hugh's shoulder. "I know, but you'll thank me by the time this evening is over."

"I think it's more probable that I'll want to kill you by the time this evening is over, but whatever. Let's go. I want to go home, and I know you won't drive me back until I do whatever you have in mind."

"Good boy."

Hugh walked behind Sean, who was almost bouncing on the balls of his feet. They were allowed inside. Hugh jerked back at the onslaught of things that hit him at once—the music, but also the smell of too many bodies pressed together, of alcohol, sweat, of a dozen other things that he didn't like. He eyed the door, but he knew he wouldn't be able to make a run for it.

So he looked around. It took him a moment to find Leon,

and when he did, he wished he hadn't. Leon was right smack in the middle of the dance floor, and he wasn't alone. He was dancing, his hands thrown around a guy's neck, the guy's thigh between Leon's. They were grinding against each other, and Leon seemed to be having fun.

Hugh wasn't.

He turned around and headed to the door, but Sean caught his wrist and pulled him back. "Where are you going?" he yelled next to Hugh's ear.

"I'm not watching him having sex or doing anything with that guy," Hugh said. That was asking too much of him. He didn't have a say in what or who Leon did, but it didn't mean he wanted to see it happened.

Sean shook his head, and to Hugh's dismay, dragged him closer to Leon. Hugh did his best to break free, but Sean's hold was hard, at least until they reached Leon. Then Sean let go and wiggled his way between Leon and the guy he was dancing with. Hugh was impressed, at least until Sean pushed Leon in Hugh's direction. Leon tripped, and Hugh acted on instinct, catching him before he could fall.

Then there he stood, with Leon in his arms, and no idea what to do.

For a moment, Leon had no idea what had happened. One moment, he was dancing with a guy he thought he could convince to go to the men's room to have sex with, and the next, he was standing in front of Hugh, with Hugh's hands on his skin. They stared at each other for a while, then Leon asked. "What are you doing here?"

Hugh shook his head. "Sean dragged me. He thought I could use an evening out." He tilted his chin toward the man who'd stepped between Leon and his now-lost one-night stand, and Leon realized it was Sean. Leon glared at him, but in truth, he didn't really care. Yes, he'd been planning to fuck the guy he'd been dancing with, but he could find someone else.

Although how he would do that with Hugh in the club, he wasn't sure.

The reason he was here was to forget everything about Hugh. He didn't want to think about him, but how was he supposed to do that with Hugh right in front of him, still holding him as if to make sure he didn't fall and hurt himself?

God, he was so sweet, and Leon wished he could deal with this differently. But he couldn't, and that meant that he should probably put some distance between himself and Hugh. It would be better for everyone, but especially for Hugh, who wouldn't get hurt if he did.

Leon wasn't sure he had it in him to reject Hugh again, though. He stepped away, but he stayed close, and he looked around. "I didn't think this was your kind of place," he said. It was hard to be heard over the music.

"It isn't. I'll be honest, I don't like crowds, so this isn't a place I usually come to when I go out."

"Do you want to leave?"

To Leon's surprise, Hugh hesitated, then shook his head. "Not yet. I just found you."

Leon had no idea what that meant, but he grinned and grabbed Hugh's hand. Leon would have a hard time letting go of Hugh once this was over, but maybe for a moment, he could enjoy it. It wouldn't last long anyway. Hugh was probably going to bolt eventually and leave Leon behind, just the way he should.

Leon was surprised to see that Hugh was going along with it, especially after Leon stepped closer to dance with him. Hugh's expression would have been funny in any other circumstance, but right now, Leon couldn't find it in himself to find it funny. If anything, the confusion and embarrassment and hint of fear made Hugh look adorable, and that shouldn't have been possible. Hugh was a grown adult. He had broad shoulders and looked reliable and serious. He *wasn't* adorable, yet in a sense, he was.

And he obviously wasn't used to dancing in a club.

Leon moved his body against Hugh's, making sure they didn't touch too often—as much as that was possible in this kind of place. But when they were pressed together, Leon could feel every single angle and plane of Hugh's body. He was pretty sure he could also feel Hugh's erection pressing against him, but of course, he didn't mention it. The last thing he wanted was to embarrass Hugh even more, and he didn't want this moment to end, which was what would happen if he did.

They danced. Leon wasn't sure for how long, but he felt safe wrapped in Hugh's arms. He knew this dance wouldn't lead to anything more, and it was both unsettling and soothing. Hugh didn't expect anything from Leon. Leon was sure of that, especially after their conversation in the car. He was just dancing with Leon.

Then suddenly, he wasn't. Hugh let go of Leon as if the contact had burned him, or maybe as if he realized it was wrong, and he turned around. He pushed his way through the crowd until he disappeared. Leon was still staring after him, trying to make a decision and feeling lost. Should he go after Hugh, or should he leave him alone? He had no idea what had happened, and while he was curious, it might be better for him to stay back. He was worried, though. He wanted to help, even though he wasn't sure he could.

Sean pushed him. "Go after him!" he yelled in Leon's ear. He was still holding the guy Leon had been dancing with, but the man didn't seem disappointed by the change in his dance partner. Leon was conflicted about, well, everything, but his entire body was telling him to go after Hugh and check on him.

So he did. He followed Hugh's path through the crowd, but of course, Hugh was nowhere to be seen. Since he wasn't crazy about clubs and crowds, Leon headed outside of the club, to the parking lot. It was the quietest place he would be able to find Hugh, and sure enough, that was where Leon found him.

Hugh was leaning against one of the cars, but Leon didn't recognize it, so he thought it might be Sean's. Hugh looked up when he heard Leon, and he didn't look happy. Leon wasn't sure what to do with that or how he felt about it, but his best bet was to ignore it.

"You should get back inside," Hugh said. "Go have fun."

"We were having fun together."

"We were. But I told you I don't like crowds, and I don't like dancing. I think I'm going to wait for Sean here. You should go back and maybe tell him, if you manage to pry him away from the guy you were dancing with."

Leon crossed his arms over his chest. "What if I don't want to?"

Hugh was still looking away from him, and his back was ramrod straight. "Why wouldn't you want to? You were very clear. You told me you didn't want anything to do with me, and I'm trying to respect that. I'm okay. I promise. You can find someone else to dance with. I'm sure you'll have plenty of volunteers."

Something was happening here, and Leon didn't understand what it was. He wanted to find out, though. That meant he wasn't going anywhere. He could tell that he was on the brink of something huge happening, and he wanted to throw himself off the cliff and find out what it was. It was both terrifying and exhilarating at the same time.

"Tell me what's going on," he said.

"Trust me. You don't want to know."

"I wouldn't ask if I didn't. Talk to me, Hugh. Something is wrong, and I want to help." It was probably the wrong decision to make, but Leon couldn't find it in himself to step away. He didn't seem to be able to respect his own rules when it came to Hugh, and he had no idea whether or not it was a good thing. This could end in a disaster, but he couldn't back down.

CHAPTER FIVE

Hugh didn't know what to do. He knew what he *wanted* to do, which was turn around, drag Leon into his arms, and kiss him senseless. He knew better than to do that, though. He suspected Leon wouldn't take it well, even though he was obviously worried about Hugh.

So that was out. What other options did Hugh have? He could leave, but he didn't want to disappoint or hurt Leon. He could tell him the truth, which was why he was here after all. He knew that everyone, even his brothers he hadn't talked to yet and his parents, would tell him to tell Leon about shifters and that they were mates. It would be the right thing to do, and Hugh agreed. Even if Leon ended up rejecting him, he still deserved to know what was happening. It wouldn't be fair to him to hide things from him, especially things that were so important.

But how was Hugh supposed to confess all of that to Leon? He had never told anyone he was a shifter. He didn't have many friends to begin with, and even those he did have, he wasn't close with, certainly not close enough to tell them about his swan form. How had Curtis revealed it to Manuel? He'd never explained it to Hugh, but everyone knew it had gone well. Manuel was still around, and Hugh doubted he would leave anytime soon.

Hugh wished he could say the same, but he had no idea how things would go. He wouldn't find out until he said the words, but they were stuck in his throat. Fear was keeping them there, and Hugh needed to either go home or find a way around that.

"Hugh?"

Leon's voice was so soft and gentle that it made Hugh's chest tighten. Hugh wanted this. He wanted Leon in his life, forever. If they couldn't be together, he would make-do with being friends, although having to watch Leon be with other people would be hell. Hugh was ready to do it, though, if it meant having a relationship with his mate. It wasn't even because Leon was his mate. It was because Leon was Leon— loveable, gentle, caring, lights up the room, Leon.

Hugh sucked in a breath and looked straight at Leon. "I'm a swan shifter. That means I can turn into a swan. Also, you're my mate, and yes, it does mean the same thing as in the movies and books."

There. Hugh had said it. He'd confessed everything, and now, he only had to wait to find out what Leon would say and how he would react.

Hugh held his breath and looked at his mate. He couldn't tell what Leon was thinking, and it was worrying. It was also causing him to be anxious, and he didn't like it. He wanted to go home. He didn't want to find out what Leon would say about this anymore. He didn't want to have to face rejection, but he was done being afraid.

But instead of running away, instead of yelling that it wasn't possible and that Hugh was lying, or maybe that Hugh was a monster, Leon cocked his head and stared at Hugh. "Are you okay?" he asked.

Hugh could have slapped himself. He should have seen this coming. Leon was too nice to tell Hugh he was lying or that he didn't believe him, but that niceness meant he would want to make sure that Hugh was okay. "Did you hear what I said?" Hugh asked. He wanted to be sure before he tried to convince Leon that he wasn't hallucinating.

"Of course I did. That's why I'm asking you if you're

feeling okay. Did you drink before coming to the club? It's all right if you did. You're here to have fun. I just want to be sure you're feeling fine."

Hugh shook his head. "I'm not lying, and I'm not delusional. I *am* a swan shifter. If you don't believe me, you should call Manuel. My entire family can shift into swans, and he knows about it. He's seen Curtis shift."

Leon shook his head, and Hugh knew he didn't believe him. "I think I should get Sean," Leon said. He didn't move, though, and Hugh hoped it meant he was willing to listen.

Hugh raked a hand through his hair. It hadn't been combed to begin with, and he was sure he looked a fright right now. "I'm not delusional," he repeated. "I'm a swan shifter, and you're my soulmate, Leon." He needed to find a way to get Leon to believe him, but he could only think of one thing that would make that happen, and it was a last resort.

"I'm sure you believe everything you're saying," Leon said slowly.

Hugh had enough. He knew that no matter how many times he repeated the same things, Leon wouldn't believe him. He wouldn't believe him because of how unbelievable he sounded, and Hugh didn't blame him. He might wish that Leon didn't treat him like he might snap at any second, but he wasn't sure he would have believed himself if he'd been in Leon's shoes. He might not have told this to anyone else before, but he could imagine what Leon was thinking right now. This could flip his life around, and it was safer to think that Hugh wasn't all there and was hallucinating.

But even though he understood, it didn't mean he wanted to do this. He'd told Leon his truth. He wasn't planning on shifting in the middle of the parking lot where anyone could walk up on them. He was a little hurt that Leon didn't believe him, even though he realized how strange it sounded. Leon was his mate. If he didn't believe Hugh, who would?

Hugh raised his hands. He wanted Leon to believe him, but he was tired. "I'm going home," he said. "I told you what I had to tell you. Now you're the one who has to make decisions. I've done my part."

"What do you mean?"

But Hugh was done explaining. He was done confessing about himself. He wanted to go home, lock himself in his apartment, and not open for anyone, not even Sean or his mom. Of course, he wouldn't be allowed to do that, but he could still go home right now. He would have to grab a cab, but that was okay.

He looked around, then headed toward the sidewalk, or at least, he tried to. Long fingers wrapped around his wrist, dragging him back, and Hugh reacted on instinct.

He shifted.

It was stupid. He was still dressed, which meant that as soon as he was in his swan form, he was in trouble because he was wrapped in fabric. He didn't have hands to untangle himself, either. He tried to pull on the clothes with his beak, but it wasn't helping, and his webbed feet wouldn't do any better.

Hugh had made a mistake, perhaps the biggest mistake in his life. Not only had he told Leon that shifters were real, but he'd also panicked and shifted in front of him. He couldn't believe this was happening. He was thirty-five years old. He shouldn't be shifting in panic anymore. He was past that, or at least, he'd thought he was. Leon seemed to trigger all of Hugh's instincts, though, and the flight-or-fight one was working just fine. Hugh had tried to flee, and now he was stuck.

He wriggled, hoping to at least manage to get his head out. He had no idea how Leon was taking this, but he might have run away, or maybe he was in shock. Hugh couldn't count on him, not when he didn't know what was happening.

"Stay still," a soft voice said.

No matter how much he wanted to, Hugh knew he couldn't obey. He couldn't risk it. He didn't know what was going through Leon's head right now, and while he hoped it was good, he couldn't be sure. Leon wouldn't be the first person to take this badly. Hugh didn't have experience with this, but he'd heard stories, and he wasn't willing to risk it.

He continued pulling with his beak and trying to open his wings, but he was stuck in his t-shirt. He supposed he should be lucky his underwear was nowhere to be seen. He had no idea why Leon wasn't running away screaming. Instead of doing that, he was trying to help Hugh, and Hugh wasn't making it easy on him.

He wanted to, but his heart was racing in his chest and his instincts were pushing at him to run away, leave Leon behind, and focus on safety. Right now, his animal instinct viewed Leon as a threat, and Hugh wasn't sure they were wrong. Leon *was* a threat, albeit not in the way most people would think.

He was a threat to Hugh's future. He was a threat to Hugh's self-esteem. It was ridiculous that a word from Leon could make or break Hugh's day and his life, but that was what being a shifter meant. Leon was Hugh's soulmate. He could hurt Hugh more than anyone else in the world, and Hugh wouldn't be able to do anything to stop him.

He could only pray that Leon *wouldn't* hurt him, but what did he know? He hadn't tried to get to know Leon. Leon hadn't tried to get to know him, either, but at least, he had the excuse that he was human and that he didn't know about soulmates. What excuse did Hugh have? None. Instead of doing what was right, Hugh had clung to his emotions, especially his fear. It had been easier than putting himself out there, and now, he was regretting it. He couldn't read Leon's tone, and he couldn't see him.

He also regretted shifting in front of Leon and especially before getting naked. He couldn't remember the last time he'd done something like this, but he was pretty sure he'd still been a teenager, and he hated it. He hated how vulnerable Leon made him feel, and he wanted it to stop.

He wasn't sure it would.

Hugh's head finally found a hole in his t-shirt, and he pushed it through. He took a deep breath, then another, and he looked around. To Hugh's surprise, Leon was still there. He was crouching next to him, his hands extended over him, but not touching him. Hugh looked at him, unsure of what to do. His body was still tangled in his t-shirt. Only his head was free, and the easiest way to solve the problem would be to shift back.

He would end up mostly naked in front of Leon if he did that, but that wasn't what scared him the most. No, what scared him was that in his human form, he would be able to answer the questions Leon no doubt had. He wouldn't have an excuse not to. Not wanting to wouldn't fly, not in this situation.

Leon had no idea what to think, and if he was honest with himself, he was pretty sure he wasn't thinking at all. His brain was frozen on the words Hugh had said, but more importantly, on the fact that Hugh had become a black swan in front of him.

Leon had thought that Hugh was already drunk, or maybe that he'd hit his head before coming to the club—and he'd been ready to tear Sean a new one for dragging his brother here in that condition. When Hugh had started saying that he was a shifter and that Leon was his mate, Leon had been sure that he was hallucinating. He'd wanted to help anyway. No matter what was going on, Hugh was a good person, and

Leon would never abandon him in the parking lot while he was talking nonsense.

Except it wasn't nonsense, was it?

Hugh had turned into a black swan. Leon couldn't deny it, not when he'd seen it with his own two eyes. It was hard to believe, almost impossible, but Leon couldn't focus on that now.

Leon didn't know what it meant or how shifters worked. He wasn't in a movie or a book. This was real life, and Leon didn't know if what he thought he knew was real or just fiction.

He didn't know what to do, so he focused on untangling Hugh from the t-shirt he was trapped in. So far, only his head had poked out of the t-shirt, and that was the smallest part of his body. He needed help, and Leon wanted to be the person who did that.

He didn't know what it meant. He didn't know if it would mean anything at all. Hugh was distraught, and Leon hated that it was his fault. He understood how hard it had been for Hugh to tell him the truth, and he wanted to reassure him, but he wasn't sure how he felt himself, so how could he? Things might have been different if they'd been alone and if Leon hadn't been terrified of someone catching them, but instead, they were in a parking lot, and Leon's heart was racing with fear and confusion. He needed to get Hugh to a safe place.

He couldn't stop thinking about the fact that Hugh had become a swan in front of him, but also about the words Hugh had said. He'd confessed he was a swan shifter, but also that Leon was his mate.

If he and Hugh were soulmates, they were meant to be together, right? And if they were meant to be together, Leon couldn't run from this, no matter how much he wanted to.

He needed to take care of Hugh and make sure he was okay before he allowed himself to freak out. It seemed that Hugh was still in there somewhere, even though Leon couldn't see him. There was intelligence in the swan's dark eyes, and Leon decided to tempt fate. He reached out with trembling fingers and stroked them down the smooth feathers of Hugh's back.

They were warm. Leon hadn't expected it, although he supposed he should have. Of course the feathers were warm. The swan, Hugh or not, was still a living being. He breathed, and he emanated warmth.

Leon's fingers were interrupted by the fabric Hugh was still wrapped in, and now that Hugh had calmed down, Leon took the opportunity to help him out of the t-shirt. It was fairly easy now that Hugh wasn't panicking anymore.

"Here you go," Leon said once he had the t-shirt off. He was grateful that the jeans and underwear wouldn't be a problem, and he grabbed them as he got to his feet. Hugh might not need them right now, but he would eventually, and Leon would have them when it happened.

Leon looked down. The swan was impressive now that he could see it entirely. The top of his head reached Leon's waist, and his long neck was incredibly graceful. Leon wanted to touch him again, but he didn't dare. He needed to talk to Hugh, the human one.

"What the fuck is going on?"

Leon jerked so hard at the sound of Sean's voice that he dropped Hugh's clothes. He leaned down to gather them again, and when he straightened, Sean was already halfway to him, and Hugh was hiding behind his legs. He looked around, wondering what was about to happen. Since Hugh was a shifter, chances were that Sean was, too. Unless it worked like werewolves? Had a swan shifter bitten Hugh, and that was why he was a shifter now? Leon *really* needed to talk to someone.

"Leon?" Sean called out again.

Leon rubbed his face. "I'm fine," he told Sean, but of

course, Sean was having none of it.

He stopped once he was in front of Leon and looked at him. "You don't look okay. What happened? Whose clothes are these? And where is Hugh.?"

Leon swallowed and stepped to the side to reveal Hugh, still in his swan form. He almost laughed when Hugh moved with him, trying to stay out of sight. Clearly Hugh didn't want to talk to his brother or for Sean to see him, and Leon wondered why. Maybe Sean wasn't a shifter after all. Maybe no one but Leon knew about this. That couldn't be right, though. Leon didn't remember Hugh's exact words, but he'd said something about Manuel being aware of this, right?

Sean looked down and swore. "For fuck's sake, Hugh. What did you do? Why did you think that shifting in this place was a good idea?"

Leon frowned. He didn't like the way Sean was talking to his brother, especially since Hugh couldn't answer him.

Sean leaned down to take Hugh into his arms, but Leon moved until he was between them again. Sean arched a brow at him and straightened, and Leon was grateful that he waited for him to speak, even though he still had no idea what he was about to say.

Instead of talking, he thrust Hugh's clothes into Sean's arms, then leaned down to take Hugh himself.

He wasn't sure how to do that. He'd never had pets, and swans didn't qualify as pets. It was the first time he'd been this close to a swan or any kind of bird that wasn't a pigeon, and he'd never tried to grab a pigeon. He didn't want to hurt Hugh, but that might happen. Maybe Leon should let Sean pick his brother up after all.

But no. Leon could do this. He was curious, and he had a dozen questions to ask, but he wanted Hugh to feel safe first and foremost. He didn't know how he would make it happen, but maybe holding him would help.

He gently took Hugh into his arms, then hauled him up and held him close, even though he was heavier than Leon had expected. "He shifted," he told Sean.

Sean rolled his eyes. "I can see that. Why? Was he trying to show you that shifters are real?"

"He was trying to run away, I think."

Sean threw his hands in the air, almost dropping Hugh's jeans. "Of course he wanted to fly away. He always does that. As soon as there's a problem, he freaks out and tries to leave. Then he hides in his apartment and ignores everyone until we break down his door because we're worried."

Leon didn't like how Sean was talking about his brother, but who was he to say anything? Sean knew Hugh better than anyone else in the world. He certainly knew him better than Leon did.

Still, he felt he had to say something. "He'd just told me something huge, something life-changing, and not only for me. I can understand he wanted to run away, especially after I implied he was hallucinating. I don't think I would have believed him if I hadn't seen him shift, to be honest." To Leon's surprise, Hugh's neck twisted, and he looked at Leon. Leon cleared his throat. He didn't know what else to say, and now wasn't the right moment or place. "We should probably leave. Some people might have questions if they head to their car and find two men standing around, one of which is holding a black swan."

Sean chuckled. "You're probably not wrong. Okay, how about this? I'm going to drive Hugh home. You can sit in the back seat with him in your arms, or on the seat next to you. You can ask me any question you want to ask as I drive. Once we leave him at his apartment, I can drive you home, too. Unless you'd rather grab a cab?"

There was no way Leon would do that. He was shaky, and he wasn't about to let go of Hugh's warm body. "You can drive. But I'm warning you—I have a lot of questions." That was an understatement if Leon had ever heard one, and he hoped Sean was ready, because he wouldn't let him go before he got at least some of the answers he was seeking.

Hugh knew he should shift back, but he didn't feel like it. He didn't want to leave Leon's arms. He felt oddly safe in them, and he knew it wouldn't last. Eventually, he would have to answer Leon's questions, although Sean was doing a good job of it for now.

So Hugh stayed in his swan form, his neck wrapped around the back of Leon's, his face tucked close to his wing, and listened as Sean explained to Leon what was happening.

"So what *are* shifters?" Leon asked.

"Exactly what you think. We're not werewolves, so we don't turn only with the full moon, and we can't bite people and turn them into shifters, but for the rest, it's pretty much the same. We can shift back and forth without a problem and any time we want."

"And your animal is a swan."

"In our family's case, yes. Dad is human, though."

"He is?"

Leon hadn't met their parents yet, and Hugh didn't expect that to change anytime soon. He still didn't know what Leon thought about all of this, especially about the mate bit. He sounded interested in the shifter part of the story, but that didn't mean anything. Everyone was interested in the shifter part. People were curious and fascinated when they found out about it, but Hugh suspected things would become harder when Leon got to the mates part.

"Yes. He and Mom told us the story of how they met and how he found out she was a swan shifter hundreds of times. To make it short, he was terrified of her in the beginning, but he got used to it, and it's a good thing, since his seven sons are all swan shifters."

"I can imagine what he went through."

"I can imagine you're feeling pretty much the same he did back then, but don't worry about him. He's perfectly fine and happy. He and Mom have been together for decades, and that's never going to change."

There was a pause, then Leon's arms tightened around Hugh, and he asked, "Because they're mates?"

"Yeah, exactly. They're mates, just like you and Hugh."

Hugh glared even though Sean couldn't see him. He wanted to slap his brother so he would stop reminding Leon of the mate thing. He didn't want to talk about it. He didn't want to be rejected.

"Does being soulmates mean the same thing as it does in the movies and books? You know, that they're perfect for each other, that they'll fall in insta-love, things like that?" Leon asked.

"Pretty much. I know you have questions about that, but while I'm more than happy to answer them, I think you should ask Hugh."

"I think I like to stay with him for a while, just to make sure he's fine."

"He is, I promise. But of course you can stay with him. I'm sure he would be happy about it."

Hugh untucked his face from his wing and turned his head around to glare at Sean without unhooking it from Leon's neck. Sean didn't see him, since he was driving and Leon and Hugh were in the backseat, but from the way he was grinning, he knew what he was doing, and Hugh wanted to slap him.

"Hey," Leon murmured.

Hugh blinked at him, wondering if he should hide again. He didn't know what Leon wanted, and he was terrified of the unknown and of how strongly he felt about all of this.

"You know, you're scaring me a bit," Leon said. "Sean, is it easy for you guys to shift back to human form?"

"Yep. I know humans don't have anything to compare it to, but think about it like putting on your clothes and taking them off. It takes less time than that, but yes, it's just that easy."

"Then why isn't Hugh shifting back?"

Sean snorted loudly. "I bet he's embarrassed."

"Why should he be?"

"I don't know. I'm pretty sure he wasn't planning on telling you all of this. He probably doesn't want to face the consequences. And he *definitely* wasn't planning on shifting in the middle of the club parking lot. That much, I'm sure of."

He was right. Hugh knew that eventually, he and Leon would have to talk, but in the meantime, this felt safer. For whatever reason, Leon was worried about him. He wasn't pushing him away. He wasn't telling him that he needed to go home and never see Hugh again. Hugh wasn't sure if all of that would end once they talked. He hoped not, but it seemed that Leon was more comfortable with his swan form than with his human one, and if that was what kept Leon by his side, he would stay a swan as long as he could.

"Here you go," Sean said as he stopped the car. He peered out the window at the apartment building. "I should probably help you get upstairs. Are you sure you want to stay, Leon? Because I can drive you home. I promise you Hugh will be okay. He'll probably pout for a bit, but he won't have a problem shifting back."

Hugh tucked his head against Leon's neck again, praying that Leon would say no. He wanted Leon to stay, of course. He wasn't sure they should talk yet, but he didn't want to lose this. For the first time in what felt like forever, he was right where he belonged. He felt like this was his place in life, and he didn't want to move.

"I can call a cab later. I want to be sure he's fine," Leon said, holding Hugh against his chest.

Sean snorted, and Hugh waited for him to say something rude, but instead, he opened his door and left the car. He walked to the back seat, grabbing the bundle of Hugh's clothes and gesturing at Leon to get out of the car. "I can carry him," he said, reaching out. "It wouldn't be the first time."

Leon's fingers dug into Hugh's feathers. "I can do it. He's heavier than I expected, but not so much that I can't do this."

"I just wanted to be sure you know you didn't have to do it."

"I know. But this is so incredibly weird, and I'm having a hard time wrapping my mind around it. Having him in my arms, feeling so solid and *here*, helps."

"Whatever you need. I'm sure Hugh doesn't mind."

Of course, Hugh didn't mind. If he had it his way, he would stay in Leon's arms forever. He would have to shift eventually, but not yet.

"I hope he doesn't. I have to admit I'm curious. I've never been this close to a swan, and I doubt I ever will be. It's . . . an experience."

He wasn't wrong. Real swans could be assholes. Hugh understood why they bit and stayed away from humans most of the time, but in Leon's case, he didn't feel it was fair. Of course, he was no doubt biased about it. Leon was his mate, and Hugh could think like a human being. He understood Leon wasn't a danger. Real swans couldn't.

He leaned back slightly and nodded so Leon knew he was more than okay with this, then buried his face against Leon's neck again. He would have smiled if he could have when Leon's fingers touched the feathers of his neck and glided down.

Leon was in awe. He wanted to continue touching Hugh, and he knew that the best way to make that happen was to continue to talk. For whatever reason, it seemed like Hugh relaxed listening to Leon's voice, and it wasn't a problem for him, not now that they were alone in Hugh's apartment.

Sean had unlocked the door and pointed out where the kitchen and bathroom were—and of course, Hugh's bedroom. He hadn't come in, and as soon as the door had closed behind him, Leon had made a beeline for the bedroom. He was sitting on the bed right now, Hugh still in his arms.

"You're gorgeous," he murmured. "You know, I don't think I've ever seen a black swan. Are all of your brothers black? What about your mom?"

Leon thought black swans were much prettier than white ones. The thought made him giggle—did white feathers get dirty more quickly, or did that only go for fur? He wasn't about to ask, but the thought did flicker in his mind for a second.

Hugh wiggled, making it known that he wanted out of Leon's arms, and Leon obeyed. He gently put Hugh down on the bed next to him and waited to find out what was about to happen.

To his surprise, Hugh shifted. Leon's eyes widened, and he looked away, because Hugh was entirely naked, which wasn't a surprise, but still.

"I can go grab your clothes from where Sean left them, if you want." Leon started to get up, but he didn't feel steady on his feet.

"You can look. I covered all the offensive bits with the blanket," Hugh said.

Those words made Leon frown, and he looked at Hugh. "Offensive?"

Hugh shrugged and looked away. "You know what I mean."

He'd wrapped the blanket around his shoulders, but it didn't cover his legs, and Leon's gaze was attracted to the sight of so much skin and hair. He wanted to touch, but he realized now wasn't the moment. "I don't think I do, but we can ignore that conversation for the huge one already waiting for us to get to it. Sean told me about shifters."

Hugh nodded. "I'm sure you have more questions, and that you want to know about soulmates."

He wasn't wrong. Leon was *dying* to know about soulmates. From what he knew, it sounded like something he would love, but he needed to be sure before doing or saying anything.

He smiled at Hugh. "Tell me about soulmates, then. I have more questions about shifters, but they can wait. I want to know about this part."

Hugh grimaced, and while Leon expected him to brush the question away, he didn't. "Soulmates are what you think of when you say the word. Our two souls belong together. Shifters have a good sense of smell, especially when it comes to their mate. I knew as soon as I smelled you in Curtis's kitchen that you were mine."

Leon frowned. "You mean during the move? Is that how you realized I was your mate, through scent?"

"Yes. I know I should have told you, but I was in shock, and after the conversation we'd had in the car . . ."

Leon cringed. He'd told Hugh he didn't date, ever. He hadn't given Hugh the time to speak or to explain, and now, he regretted it. "So does it mean that soulmates never hurt each other?"

Hugh shook his head. "Of course we hurt each other. I'm sure some of them say stupid things, and even though there's a bond there, it doesn't mean we have to do anything. I'm pretty sure that some soulmates decide not to be together."

"Then why is it a thing? If we don't *have* to be together, why are we mates?"

"Being mates is just an indication, I think. It's the way the world has of telling you that this person in front of you will make you happy if you allow them to and if you're good to them. But just like every other relationship, you have to work on that. I would never hurt you intentionally, but I've been known to say or do stupid things, and I know that we'll hurt each other one way or another, just like every couple. But we have an advantage over those other couples. We fit together. We think similarly. That will help."

Leon's father should have loved him unconditionally, but he hadn't. Instead, he'd kicked him out of the house as soon as Leon had come out to him, and he'd told him exactly what he thought of him being gay. He'd yelled at Leon that he was an abomination, that he went against God and was a child of the devil. His dad had never been religious, and Leon had been stunned.

He'd been even more stunned when his mother had divorced his father for what he'd done. She hadn't stayed with him after that night. When Leon's father had kicked him out, his mother had come with him, and she'd taken him to a motel for the night.

Now, Leon found himself hoping that he could have that unconditional love, the love he'd been seeking for so long, with Hugh. If he and Hugh were soulmates, that meant that Hugh was the one person who wouldn't hurt him, right?

Leon knew that was unrealistic. He had hurt people he cared about, and they had hurt him. Manuel had said a few things that hurt Leon, and he'd no doubt done the same. That didn't mean they weren't friends, though. They were, and Leon couldn't help but imagine what his relationship with Hugh could be like.

His first instinct was to say no and leave, then stay away and make sure Hugh and everything he brought with him didn't come anywhere close to him ever again. It was what Leon wanted.

Except it wasn't. When Leon forced himself to calm down and think, he realized he wanted to give Hugh a chance. Hugh would love him, even though his father couldn't. But Leon was terrified, and he didn't know what was next. He didn't know if he could allow Hugh in, no matter how hard he tried.

What he *did* know was that he could have something precious like what Manuel and Curtis had.

The thought made him frown. "Are Manuel and Curtis mates?"

Hugh smiled. "They are."

"Dammit. I can't believe Manuel didn't tell me about this. He knows you guys are all shifters?"

"He does. Curtis told him when they saved that puppy."

Leon remembered it. Curtis had wanted to keep the puppy, but Manuel was allergic. They were thinking about getting a cat now, and Leon couldn't believe he hadn't realized what was going on between them. They weren't merely boyfriends. They were mates. Soulmates. "Is being soulmates the reason they're moving in together already?"

"Probably. I mean, when you let your soulmate in, things usually go fast. You fall in love in a matter of weeks and usually stay in love for decades, like my parents. Unless something happens and one of you changes dramatically, your souls fit together perfectly. My parents are still together, even after more than forty years, and they still love each other like the first day."

Leon smiled at that. "How do you know that? You weren't born."

"I wasn't. But I'm thirty-five, and in the past thirty-five years, I've always seen them together. They're a strong couple. They fight, just like every other couple, but you can feel the love between them."

And that was what Leon and Hugh could have. It would take work, just like any relationship. Hugh probably wasn't wrong about that, and Leon didn't know if he could do it. He wasn't a relationship kind of guy.

But he wanted to try. For the first time in forever, he wanted to give this a chance. He wanted to see if he and Hugh really could work together as well as Hugh thought they could. He wanted that love and that happiness the bond between them promised.

He just had to deal with the fear first, and he wasn't sure he could do that, no matter how much he wanted to.

CHAPTER SIX

Hugh was freaking out, and he wasn't sure what to do about it. When it came to Leon, he was never sure what to do. He didn't know whether or not he liked it, but he supposed he needed to get used to it. He and Leon were starting their relationship—if they could even call it that for now—but if Hugh had his way, it would last for a long time, or rather, forever. That meant that he needed to get used to feeling unsettled and to the butterflies in his stomach every time he thought about his mate.

He and Leon had kept in touch after that night. Leon had slept in Hugh's bed, while Hugh had taken the couch. He'd wanted to stay with Leon, of course, but it was too soon for that. Leon had no doubt needed space, and Hugh had done his best to give him just that.

All in all, Leon had taken things well. He'd had questions, of course, but Hugh had expected them, and he hadn't been surprised. He *was* surprised by the fact that Leon kept texting him, though. When Leon had asked him for his phone number the morning after Hugh had shifted in front of him, Hugh had been stunned. Leon hadn't run away screaming for the hills after finding out about shifters and mates, but that didn't mean he wanted all that implied.

Being mates was different from being boyfriends, and it was a huge commitment. Even Hugh wasn't sure he was ready for it, and he was the shifter. He could only imagine how Leon was feeling.

A knock on the door made him jerk. He'd been trying to

work, but all his thoughts were on Leon, and he was grateful for the distraction. He couldn't help but wonder if maybe Leon was visiting, although he knew that couldn't be the case. Leon would have told him about it. They might not have talked much yet after their evening together, but Leon was an enthusiastic texter.

Hugh's stomach felt weird as he opened the door. He grinned, just in case, but his excitement lasted only a few seconds. Then he realized that his brother was there, no doubt to ask him what was going on, and he could do without his questions.

"Curtis. What do you want?" he asked.

Curtis arched a brow. He looked happy, more settled than Hugh could remember him, and Hugh was relieved and happy for him. He hadn't known Curtis' ex well, but he and everyone else in their family had been able to tell that the guy wasn't the right one for Curtis. Manuel was, more than anyone else in the world could be. They were mates, and now that they were together and settling down, Curtis looked years younger. There was a spring in his step and a smile always on his lips, and Hugh wasn't sure whether he found it annoying or amusing.

"I can't visit my big brother?" Curtis asked.

"Not when I'm working."

"You've done a lot of that in the past few days?"

He knew. Hugh didn't know if Sean had spilled the beans or if Leon had talked to Manuel, but most probably, both had happened. "I did. In fact, I was working just now. What did you want?"

Curtis rolled his eyes. "To talk to you. Can I come in?"

"Of course." There was a twinge of worry in Hugh's chest. "Everything okay?" he asked as he stepped aside.

Curtis walked in. "Yep. Manuel sent me."

Hugh relaxed. "He wants you to interrogate me."

"I think he mostly wants to make sure you won't hurt Leon."

Hugh closed the door and looked at his brother. "I'm not planning to."

"But it will happen. There's not much Manuel or anyone else can do about it, but he's still worried. I guess Leon's been through a lot, and Manuel is a mother hen. He wants to be reassured that you're not playing around or something."

"Of course not. Leon is my mate." Hugh was both annoyed and touched. He was grateful that Leon had a friend in his corner. He also knew Curtis wasn't wrong. Hugh knew that both he and Leon would eventually end up hurt, and that was okay, or at least, it was something they needed to deal with. They needed to do it *without* his brother and his mate sticking their noses into it, though. "Tell him that we're dealing with it. He doesn't need any details."

Curtis flopped onto the couch and grimaced. "I know he doesn't need details, and trust me, I don't want them. I want him to be able to sleep at night."

It was annoying. Hugh couldn't deny that. But Manuel was in Hugh's life to stay, both because he was his brother's mate, and because he was Hugh's mate's best friend. "We're dealing with it," he repeated. "We haven't talked again, but we've kept in touch, and we're taking our time." Mostly because it looked like neither of them had any idea what to do, but also because the last thing Hugh wanted was to push Leon too hard and fast. Leon had reacted well to what Hugh had told him, but what was to say he wouldn't freak out if Hugh pushed?

Curtis grinned. "You don't want to talk about it. That's fine. Manuel will have to get used to that."

"How do you do it?" Hugh asked.

Curtis frowned as Hugh sat on the edge of the coffee table. The table creaked, but Hugh knew it wouldn't break. "What do you mean?"

"You and Manuel, or you and anyone else you had a relationship with for that matter. How do you do it? You know I'm not the best at being social, and apparently, that includes with my mate."

"You told him about shifters and mates."

"You know I have." Because if there was one thing Leon would have told Manuel, it was that. He'd probably called him from the elevator when he'd left Hugh's apartment to yell at him for keeping shifters a secret from him. "I meant having a relationship. Both Leon and I are so insecure, it feels like we might never trust each other, and I can't imagine we can make a relationship work like that."

Curtis frowned. "Insecure? I know there's some stuff in Leon's past, but what about you? Why are you insecure?"

"I'm boring," Hugh blurted out. He regretted saying the words almost immediately, but they were out now.

Curtis sat up. "What?"

Hugh sighed and looked away. "I'm boring. I know I am. I work from home and wear sweats most days. Even when I'm not working, I don't like to go out. I like staying home where it's quiet and I don't have to deal with people."

"Did Leon tell you that? That you were boring?"

"No, of course not. But you know me, and you know him. He's so colorful and happy. He likes people. He likes to go *dancing*, for fuck's sake. He's so fun and everything, and I'm the exact opposite. What if I'm too boring for him? What if he wants better? He certainly *deserves* better." Hugh didn't want to think about Leon with someone else, but he knew it might happen. Being mates didn't mean they would be happy forever after. It wasn't a guarantee.

"You have to talk to him." Curtis raised a hand before Hugh could protest. "I know you don't like that idea, and honestly, I don't think anyone likes to talk about feelings. It makes us vulnerable. But you and Leon need to talk about this and everything else. It's the only way to make your relationship work, Hugh. You just said that you're both insecure. That's not going to be easy to get over. You need to be honest with each other and open to having this kind of conversation. Tell him how you feel. Allow him in and show him that you're there for him and that you want him in your life."

It felt like an impossible task. "I don't know if I can do it. Maybe it would be better for him to find someone else."

Curtis shook his head. "Manuel never told me why Leon is the way he is, and unless Leon wants to tell me, I'm not going to ask. But from what I know of him, he doesn't trust people. That's why he doesn't have relationships. And you, on the other hand, feel like you're not good enough. That's heavy stuff, Hugh. You won't solve it by ignoring it or running away. If you want to be with Leon, and I hope you do, because you guys are mates and can be happy together. You need to face this head-on."

Curtis was right. Even though the thought was terrifying, Hugh needed to explain this to Leon. Would he be able to, though? Or would he lose Leon before their relationship began?

Leon was surprised how excited he was to see Hugh again. He was aware that things could still go wrong, but for the first time since he could remember — probably since ever, and since his father had kicked him out — he had hope.

It would be easy to go back to his own thoughts, but he needed to force himself to focus on what he knew. Soulmates were perfect for each other, and they were forever. He could have that with Hugh if he gave Hugh a chance, and that was what he'd been trying to do. He wasn't sure it was enough, but he supposed he would find out. And if it wasn't, he would work harder.

He hadn't thought anything would ever change his mind about relationships. He knew he was wrong now, but before, he'd believed he would never have what Manuel had found with Curtis. He'd thought he wasn't good enough and that no one would want him, not for any length of time.

But Hugh wanted him. It might be because of the mate bond, but it was a start, and Leon hoped he would be able to make it work and fall in love with him. He had to, right? Because he and Hugh were mates, and that meant that no one was better for Hugh than Leon. They would never find someone they fit better with, and even when he thought about it, Leon had a hard time believing it, but he knew it was the truth.

He flopped onto his mattress and grabbed his phone. He and Hugh had been exchanging texts since the night Hugh had shifted in front of Leon, and Leon loved it. It was a way for them to speak without meeting face to face and without letting their insecurities and embarrassment take over. Leon didn't like phone calls, so that was out, but he found that texting allowed him to let himself go and express feelings he wouldn't be able to say out loud.

He and Manuel had talked about this and a lot of other things. Leon had yelled at Manuel for not telling him about shifters, but Manuel had pointed out that he'd been afraid. He and Curtis had only met recently, and he'd just discovered the shifter world. He didn't know much about it himself, so how could he have told Leon about it?

Leon didn't agree. He thought Manuel should have told him about Curtis, at the very least. Curtis wasn't just Manuel's boyfriend. He was his mate, which was one of the reasons they were already moving in together. Leon liked to think that he would have accepted everything, although he did understand why Manuel had been hesitant.

This wasn't the kind of thing he could tell someone over a beer. Manuel knew how reluctant Leon was when it came to relationships, and he'd been afraid this would change the relationship between them. He shouldn't have been. Leon had a hard time believing that shifters were a thing, but he liked it. He liked the existence of soulmates even more.

He checked the time. Hugh hadn't yet texted, but he and Leon were seeing each other that afternoon, and Leon couldn't wait. He felt different, and he didn't know why. Maybe because he had hope? He could finally imagine a future in which he was happy and not alone. It was tentative, but it was there, and it made him feel warm and weird.

He had to be cautious, though. Everything could still be ruined, but he would do what he could to make sure that his relationship with Hugh worked. He deserved it. After so many years of one-night stands and guys who didn't care about him, who thought he was weird, or that he gave gay people a bad reputation because he wore makeup, Leon had finally found a place where he belonged. He belonged with Hugh, and he wouldn't leave, not unless someone dragged him away, and even then, he would claw his way back to Hugh.

Leon huffed at himself and rose from the bed. Now he was being dramatic. That was nothing new, of course. He was always dramatic, and Hugh would have to get used to that. Leon couldn't help but wonder if Hugh would be able to. He looked like a no-nonsense kind of man, which was as far from Leon as anyone could be. They were polar opposites, and while that worried Leon, he had to keep trust in fate or in whoever had decided that he was Hugh's soulmate. Since he was, it meant that even though they were different, they would work together.

He had to believe that.

He checked his reflection in the mirror once again. He'd

been ready for about half an hour, which was a small miracle for him. Usually he was late for everything. His mother always teased him that he would have been late at his own birth if she hadn't had a cesarean. But today, Leon wouldn't be late. He wouldn't make Hugh wait.

His hair fell perfectly on his forehead, and his lipstick was neutral enough that he could wear it during the afternoon. He knew that if he stayed home, he would obsess over the way he looked, and he might change his clothes a few more times. He couldn't afford to do that, so he decided to head out. There was nothing else he could do in the house anyway. Besides, he knew Hugh wouldn't care. He liked Leon for who he was, not for his makeup or his clothes.

Leon's phone pinged as he left his building. It was Hugh, and Leon smiled instantly. He chuckled at his reaction. When had he become so sweet on Hugh? He barely knew the man, even though they'd been texting for a while. He hoped to change that, though, which was why he was headed out on a date. He, Leon, was going on a date.

His mother would laugh her ass off if she knew. She'd also be happy for him, though, and it was one more thing that pointed to the fact that he was doing the right thing.

He opened the text, then frowned. It was Hugh, but the text wasn't a good one, or at least, it could become a bad one if Leon allowed it.

I'm scared, Hugh had written. *I don't usually do relationships. I know you don't, either, and I'm afraid that this won't work.*

Leon had to be careful about how he answered that. He didn't want to freak Hugh out, but he also didn't want to lie to him.

You're right. I don't have experience with relationships, either, he answered. *It's easier to keep people away than risk getting hurt. I have a painful past, and I don't want it to happen again. I think that the fear of being hurt has held me back, though.*

He sent the message, then waited, holding his breath.

Hugh's answer came after only a few moments. *I'm sorry you were hurt. I understand why you're afraid to put your heart out there.*

Leon didn't want to tell Hugh about his father, but maybe it would be easier to do that by text. *My father kicked me out when I was seventeen after I came out to him. I was lucky, because my mother divorced him and stuck by my side, but it still hurts to this day. He couldn't accept me for who I was, even though he was my father and he should have been one of the two people in the world to love me unconditionally.*

He sent the text before he could change his mind. He wanted Hugh to know him, his past, and why he would no doubt put distance between them every so often. He wanted Hugh to understand why he was so insecure and afraid.

I'm sorry that happened to you, Hugh's answer read. *It shouldn't happen to anyone, but I'm glad you had your mother.*

Leon was glad he'd had his mom, too. He was glad he still had her, but after seeing Manuel and Curtis together, and after meeting Hugh, he was starting to realize that it wasn't enough. He loved his mom and Manuel, but he wanted more.

He wanted Hugh.

Hugh was stunned — not to find out Leon had been hurt, but because Leon was telling him about it. He'd expected to have to wait a long time before Leon told him about his past. Instead, Leon had taken advantage of their text messages to tell Hugh about his father and what the man had done, just like Hugh had used them to confess he was afraid.

Hugh was angry. If he ever got his hands on Leon's father, he would throttle the man. He wasn't about to do that, of course, even though his swan was pushing at him to go. He wasn't about to act like a caveman, though. Leon knew the situation, and he'd been dealing with it for years. It wasn't Hugh's place to step in, and he had no doubt Leon would be pissed if he did so.

Besides, he had a date with Leon.

He wanted to help Leon and for their relationship to work, and he was ready to work hard to make it happen. It had been a long time since he'd been with someone for more than a few weeks, but he knew Leon was different, or at least, Hugh hoped so.

He knew he was boring. He knew their relationship wouldn't be easy.

He wanted it, though.

He slipped into the coffee shop where he and Leon had agreed to meet. It was a date, but not a dinner date. That still felt too serious for what they had. Their relationship was fragile, and they needed to take things slow. The last thing they both wanted was to send the other running. Hugh could already imagine them together, though, maybe Leon moving in with him. Or would they find a house they could choose together and share? For once in his life, Hugh was excited, and he couldn't wait to see what the future would bring.

He ordered coffee, then hesitated. He didn't know how long it would take for Leon to get there, so he didn't want to have a cold coffee for him by the time he arrived, and he also didn't want to be found empty-handed. Instead of a coffee, he bought a bottle of fruit juice, a cookie, and a brownie. That way, Leon would be able to choose what he wanted. And if he wanted a coffee, Hugh would have no problem buying it for him. He just needed to know how Leon took it, but he was ready to bet it was with a lot of sugar, and possibly one of those fancy caramel syrups.

Hugh settled at one of the tables away from the counter and stared at the door. He felt ridiculous, and he couldn't help but wonder if this was how Curtis had felt with Manuel in the beginning. Curtis had met Manuel just before Christmas, and instead of telling him what was happening and who he was, he'd bought Manuel a gift a day for the twelve days before Christmas day. It had been sweet, but it wasn't Hugh's thing.

But Hugh wasn't quite sure what his thing was. He was thirty-five, but some days he felt like he was in his early twenties. He still felt like a teenager, even though he worked, paid his bills and his taxes, and cooked every evening. He supposed that emotionally, he was still in his twenties. He'd never had a real relationship. He'd never had what he would have with Leon.

The door opened, making him jump. He looked up, and he smiled when he saw Leon stepping into the coffee shop. Since Leon hadn't seen him yet, he took his time looking at him.

He looked good. He was wearing a red t-shirt under his jacket and jeans that were so tight they might have been painted on. It was cliché, but it was true. His boots had slight heels, and his hair was all over the place, but Hugh couldn't say if it was on purpose or not. Leon also wore makeup, although not as much as he had at the club. It was more subdued but just as pretty. Leon was gorgeous, and Hugh suspected that he would find him gorgeous even without makeup, early in the morning with his eyes still sleepy.

He couldn't wait to find out.

He raised a hand and waved so Leon would see him. When Leon did, his smile widened, and he gestured at the counter. Hugh raised his brownie and cookie so Leon could see them, and he hadn't thought it possible, but Leon's smile became even wider. He nodded, but he didn't join Hugh, probably because he wanted coffee.

When Leon came, he was holding a steaming mug. He placed it on the table in front of Hugh, then took his jacket off and hooked it on the chair before sliding into it. "You're early," he said.

Hugh desperately wanted to kiss him, but he kept his distance. "I tend to be. I'm so terrified of being late that I always end up being early."

Leon laughed. "I'm the opposite. I'm always late. I don't do it on purpose but because I lose track of time. Maybe I'll start getting ready on time, but then I shower for too long, or I take long to choose my clothes, and I end up being late."

"You're not late today." If anything, he was a few minutes early.

He looked down, and to Hugh's surprise, his cheeks flushed. "I was eager to see you." He chuckled, sounding incredulous. "I can't believe it. I mean, wanting to see a guy who wants a relationship with me."

Hugh wanted to say something, but what? He wanted Leon to know he understood. He didn't want to make a mountain out of it because he doubted Leon would be happy, but he also didn't want to act as if nothing had happened.

He cleared his throat. "I don't know why your father kicked you out, if it was because you were gay or because of the way you are."

Leon snorted loudly. "You mean the makeup and everything else?"

Hugh shrugged. "What I was trying to say is that while I don't know why he did it, I also don't care. I am *never* going to kick you out. I'm not ashamed of being seen with you. If anything, I like you a lot, and I don't expect or want you to change beyond what's normal in a relationship and as time passes." He rubbed the back of his neck. "And I hope the same will go for you. I know I'm boring. I know I'm almost ten years older than you. I doubt I'll be able to change, and honestly, I don't want to, not much. I don't have anything against going out a few times with you, but I don't like clubs, for example. We're very different, you and I. I still hope we can have a relationship, but I'll understand if you don't want that."

Leon blinked. "You really don't want me to change?"

"Of course not. You're gorgeous the way you are, and more importantly, you're a good person."

"And you don't believe I give us gay people a bad reputation? That I put them to shame because of the way I look?"

Hugh couldn't help but laugh at that. "Shame? I don't see why. Bigotry would shame us. Bullying would shame us. But you? No. I know not all people think you're perfect the way I do, but it doesn't mean they're right, or that you have to change. Not everyone will be okay with the way you look and act, but do they matter? The people who love you, love you the way you are. We don't expect anything from you but for you to be yourself."

Hugh didn't have the time to move. Leon reached for him, hooking a hand behind his neck and pulling him forward. Their lips pressed together, and Hugh's eyes widened before he allowed them to slide closed. The kiss didn't last long—they were in a public place, and the table separated them and made it uncomfortable—but it was perfection.

Hugh wanted more, and from the looks of it, he thought Leon did, too. He hesitated. He wanted to say something, to acknowledge the fact that he yearned for Leon, to make Leon feel desired, but he didn't want to make a mess just when they seemed to be doing okay.

He was grateful when Leon licked his lips and said, "I know we decided to take things slow."

"We decided it was better, yes."

"It probably is, but I don't want to take things slow, Hugh. I already know what I want, and for once, I want to hope. I want to believe that even if we have sex today, you'll still be there tomorrow and the day after that. Would it be too fast for you, though? Because I can wait, even though there's nothing I want more right now than to get my hands on you."

Hugh couldn't have stopped the smile that blossomed on his face if he'd tried, and he didn't. "My apartment is close by."

Leon was nervous. He'd had a lot of sex, but this was different. This was sex with Hugh, and he knew it meant something, something important and precious that he wasn't sure he would be able to handle.

He wouldn't be able to run away after this. He wouldn't be able to leave Hugh behind. He would never do that to Hugh, but he couldn't deny he was terrified. What if things between them didn't work? What if he needed to leave even though he knew it was the wrong thing to do? He didn't know what would happen next, but he did know one thing—he wanted this desperately.

Hugh closed the door to his apartment behind himself and leaned against it. He looked at Leon, and Leon looked at him. They were silent for a moment, and Leon held his breath. Things could still go wrong. Things could *always* go wrong. There was no guarantee, and he needed to take a risk right now, a risk he hadn't taken in a long time, maybe never.

He was ready for it.

Or at least, he hoped he was. Either way, there was no going back.

He reached for Hugh at the same time Hugh reached for him. They ended up in each other's arms, and Leon tilted his head up to look at Hugh. He felt strong against Leon's body, solid, and Leon knew he would always be there for him when he needed him. He wanted this, and he needed to make sure it would happen. That meant not running away the way he felt he should.

His first instinct was to leave. He couldn't deny that. So instead, he focused on Hugh and how he felt against him. Then Hugh leaned down to kiss him, and Leon smiled.

He kissed Hugh back. It was hesitant at first, a simple

brush of the lips, once, twice, three times. Then Leon had enough, or rather, not enough. He knew he wanted this, and he hooked a hand behind Hugh's neck. He pulled him down, pressing her lips together harder, gently poking at Hugh's lips with his tongue.

He'd decided he wanted Hugh a few days earlier, but he'd never been as sure as when Hugh told him he didn't expect him to change and that he would be proud to have him by his side just the way he was. Leon didn't want to think about his father right now, but he couldn't deny that Hugh's words had helped. They'd reassured him, and even though he knew he and Hugh would hurt each other sooner or later, he knew it would never be like what his father had done.

Leon's father was supposed to be one of the two people who loved him unconditionally, and he hadn't been. Hugh would be, though. Leon was sure of that.

"We should probably move this to the bedroom," Hugh murmured.

Leon nodded, but neither of them moved. They were locked together, and he knew they would fall if they tried to walk. Going to the bedroom meant they had to step away from each other. He wasn't looking forward to it.

Hugh laughed and kissed Leon again, gently pushing him against the wall. Leon gasped, and when he hopped up to wrap his legs around Hugh's waist, Hugh didn't have a problem catching him.

This was one of the things Leon liked about being with bigger men. They could manhandle him, and in this case, he trusted Hugh completely. He knew Hugh wouldn't hurt him, so he allowed Hugh to move, putting himself in his care.

It was rocky for a second, and Leon held his breath, hoping they weren't about to end up splattered on the floor. But they didn't, and they found their way to Hugh's bedroom.

Leon had been here before, but it had been different. Hugh

had been in his swan form, and after he'd shifted, they'd talked, even though he'd been naked. This time, there was no mention of talking, just Hugh gently laying him on the bed.

Leon grinned and took off his jacket and his t-shirt, throwing it to the floor. Then his hands were on his jeans, and he didn't allow himself to slow down, even though Hugh was watching him with wide eyes — or maybe because of it. Leon wanted Hugh naked, so as soon as his boots, jeans, and underwear — and socks, because there was no way Leon was having sex with socks on — were on the floor with his t-shirt, he opened his arms and reached for Hugh.

But Hugh was more hesitant now, and Leon wondered why that was. He didn't think Hugh didn't want to do this anymore, so it had to be something else.

He was gentler when he pulled Hugh's t-shirt up, and he understood what was happening when Hugh got under the blankets as soon as he was half-naked. He still had his jeans on, and Leon wasn't surprised when he took them off under the blanket and pushed them off the side of the bed.

Leon wanted more, but he knew he had to give Hugh time and maybe reassurance, just like Hugh had with him. He propped himself up on his elbow, and when Hugh reached for him, he shook his head. "You don't have to hide," he murmured.

Hugh swallowed and wrapped his arms around Leon, pulling him close. "I don't know what you're talking about," he said against the skin of Leo's neck.

It would be easy to forget what had just happened, but Leon didn't want to. "We need to talk and be honest, remember? Don't think I didn't notice you got under the blanket before getting naked. I'm not going to push to see your body right now, but eventually, I want to. I understand that you're not comfortable with me yet, though. That's okay. But you're beautiful to me, Hugh."

Hugh shook his head. "I'm not beautiful."

"You are. You're strong, and you make me feel cherished. I won't lie—I've had a lot of sex in my life. Less now that I'm older, but when I was in my early twenties, I slept around. None of those guys felt the way you do. You're touching me as if I'm precious, and it means a lot."

"It's because you *are* precious."

That was the last thing they said. After that, they both focused on each other's bodies.

It was fun to explore Hugh's body knowing that this wouldn't be the only time it happened. It made Leon go slower, and he was grateful for that. He wanted Hugh to enjoy himself, and he wanted to enjoy himself, too, of course, but this time was different. It wasn't just a desperate search for pleasure. There *was* pleasure in everything they did, but it was more than that.

There was also care and affection, and Leon hoped, eventually, love.

The thought made him swallow hard, and he had to force himself to focus on what was happening. He didn't want Hugh to think he was freaking out, especially when he wasn't. Sometimes he was hesitant, but he could feel the same from Hugh. Still, Hugh's touch on Leon's body was firm, and when he wrapped his fingers around Leon's cock, Leon's back rose off the mattress.

Leon gasped and reached for Hugh, clutching his shoulders. "What do you want?" he asked, sounding breathless.

Hugh took his time answering, and Leon was happy about that. He wanted Hugh to enjoy this as much as he did, and it was obvious to him that they needed to take this slower than he was used to.

"I'm not sure. I want everything with you, but maybe not right now."

Leon nodded. "That's fine with me. We can make each

other feel good without pushing ourselves too far."

Hugh looked so relieved that Leon knew he'd said the right thing. He reached for Hugh again and rolled them until he was under his mate.

His mate. It was still strange to think about Hugh that way or to think the word was real. He knew it would be the same if he'd gotten married, though, so he wasn't too worried. He would get used to it. He would have to.

Leon kissed Hugh again, but it wasn't enough, and once Hugh was humping Leon's thigh, Leon knew they had to move on. He wasn't sure what he was doing, but he rolled to his side, with Hugh behind his back. They didn't have lube, but they were under the blanket, and they were sweating. Leon didn't like sweat, but he hoped that this time it would be to their advantage.

Hugh's cock slotted neatly between Leon's thighs. The head brushed against Leon's balls, making him shudder in pleasure. He wrapped himself around Leon from the back, until not a breath of air could pass between their bodies. And of course, he was thoughtful, so he took Leon's cock in his hand and moved his body at the same rhythm until Leon was on the brink of orgasm.

It wasn't exactly what Leon wanted. He wanted Hugh inside of him, claiming him that way. But he knew they needed time, and this was good, too. Maybe having a different kind of sex would help him discover Hugh. It felt good, too. They were rubbing together, and Hugh's cock was heavy between Leon's thighs. It was what they wanted, and it was enough.

Leon's pleasure peaked, and he came, babbling nonsense he hoped Hugh wasn't listening to. He wasn't quite sure Hugh hadn't heard it once they were both done, but Hugh gently brought them face to face. He was smiling, and Leon hesitated. This was usually when things went south. It was when the other guy got dressed and left, and Leon ended up alone.

But he didn't this time. Hugh gathered him into his arms even though they were both sweaty and stinky and brought him close. Leon felt incredibly vulnerable, and he didn't like it, but he knew it was necessary, so he allowed Hugh to do it. It was odd, but also good.

"Thank you," Hugh murmured.

"What are you thanking me for?"

"Trusting me. Giving me this. I know you don't do relationships, and I was surprised you were ready to do this."

Leon shrugged one shoulder. "The same goes for you. I think it's a nice first step. I can't wait to see what happens next."

Hugh smiled. "You're right. I can't wait, either."

Leon had no idea what would happen, but he wasn't lying. He couldn't wait. He wanted his happily ever after, and he had it. He was going to do everything he could not to mess things up.

Chapter Seven

"I still can't believe you didn't tell me about this," Leon said. He stuffed a piece of bread into his mouth and glared at Manuel.

Hugh had to work hard not to smile. He had to work hard most of the time, because he always felt like smiling now.

"What did you want me to do?" Manuel cried out, waving his fork around. "I couldn't just come to you and tell you, *oh, by the way, my boyfriend is a swan shifter.*"

Leon pointed a finger at him. "Yes, that's *exactly* what you should have done. We're best friends."

"I wanted to tell you. I just wasn't sure I was allowed."

Leon turned his attention to Curtis, who wiggled in his chair. Leon glared at him until Curtis said, "If it helps, I never told him not to tell you."

Leon rolled his eyes. "No, it doesn't help."

Hugh felt a bit awkward, even though it was only dinner between the four of them. It felt odd to be part of a couple and be viewed that way, but he wasn't letting Leon go, not unless Leon wanted to, and as far as Hugh was aware, he didn't.

They were still feeling their way around their relationship. They both had a lot of work to do, both on themselves and on being together. But Hugh was happier than he could ever remember being, and he knew it was because of Leon. That was not just because of his presence in his life, but also because of the changes he was making for Leon.

He probably shouldn't be changing for him. He should be changing for himself or something like that. He'd needed it even before he'd met Leon, and he wasn't going to deny it. He'd been closed-off, isolated, and that was entirely his fault. He still wasn't a sociable person, and he doubted he ever would be, even though Leon was. But that was okay. He was with people he knew, and he felt comfortable enough with them. Certainly comfortable enough to have dinner with them so Leon could be happy. Manuel was his best friend, and Hugh knew that he would be seeing a lot of him and his brother in the future.

"I can't believe you betrayed me that way," Leon dramatically said, pressing a hand to his heart.

Hugh held his breath, wondering if Manuel would be offended, but he just rolled his eyes. "Stop that. You know about shifters now, and you have your own. I don't get why you're still talking about this."

"I just wish you'd told me." Leon's voice was quieter now. "Maybe I would have met Hugh sooner."

Manuel's expression softened, and he reached for his best friend's hand over the table. "Maybe you wouldn't have. I mean, I couldn't have known that Hugh was your mate. Besides, it's not like you had to wait long to meet him. I only met Curtis a couple of months ago."

Leon shook his head, but he was smiling. "I wish I'd had a couple of months more with Hugh."

Hugh hoped he wasn't blushing. His cheeks felt hot, but he pushed the embarrassment away, or rather, he did his best to ignore it. "It wouldn't have changed anything," he said gruffly. "Now that I have you, I'm not letting you go."

Leon beamed at him. "And I'm not letting you go, either. We're stuck with each other."

Curtis guffawed. "When you say it like that, it sounds like neither of you want to be in this relationship."

Leon glared at him. "Don't talk that way to my mate. I want him. He's not going anywhere, and neither am I."

Curtis raised his hands. "That's not what I was saying. I was joking around, but all right. I won't mention it again."

Leon nodded. "Good. Because I'm not forcing him into anything, and he's not forcing me. We want to be together."

"Hell, Leon. I was just teasing you. I'm sorry."

Leon turned his attention back to Manuel, and Curtis leaned closer to Hugh. Hugh tensed, even though he didn't understand why. "He's touchy," Curtis said.

"We both are. It's still early."

"Maybe, but it looks to me like it's going well. Isn't it?"

It was. They were dating, and to Hugh's surprise, it was enough for him. He wasn't planning on moving in with Leon too soon the way Curtis had with Manuel. He wasn't his brother, and Leon wasn't Manuel.

But they saw each other almost every day, and more often than not, they shared the same bed at night. They didn't always have sex. Hugh had thought for a while that maybe Leon would get bored because of that, or that he needed sex more often, but when Leon had pointed out that even though he'd had a lot of one-night stands, he hadn't had them every day. He could do without sex, especially — and those were his words — if he got to sleep on top of Hugh during the night like Hugh was his teddy bear. The memory made Hugh blush, and he focused on his brother again.

"So things are going well?" Curtis asked, his smile widening.

"I already told you they were." At least between them. Leon's father was trying to convince his mother to talk to him, but neither she nor Leon wanted anything to do with him. He'd hurt them too much.

"I have a hard time believing Leon is okay with taking things slow. He doesn't look like that kind of guy."

"I don't think he was."

Curtis' smile softened. "But you're different."

"I am. He knows that, and he's okay with going slow." Hugh suspected the mate bond had a lot to do with that.

He loved it. He wanted Leon to know that he would never abandon him the way his father had, and the bond helped, even though Leon couldn't feel it. It wasn't a guarantee they would spend the rest of their lives together, even though they were planning to. But it meant a lot to Leon to be Hugh's mate, and it meant a lot to Hugh, too.

Hugh could tell they were both changing. He was going out more, and he was starting to believe that he wasn't as boring as he'd thought he was. As for Leon, he was relaxing. He was allowing Hugh in, and he'd stopped looking like he expected Hugh to run away any second. Sometimes they still needed their space, especially Hugh, but they made it work.

They had to, because Hugh wasn't about to leave Leon behind. He never wanted to, and he hoped Leon knew that.

He'd allowed Leon into his life, just like Leon had done with him, and they were finding their way to happiness.

Curtis knocked their shoulders together. "So, who do you think will be next?"

Hugh frowned and took a sip of water before answering. "What do you mean?"

"Well, I found my mate, then you found yours a few months later. Do you think one of our brothers will find theirs soon?"

Hugh shrugged. "We don't live in a romance novel."

"I'm betting on Laurie."

Hugh barked out a laugh. "Laurie? I don't think so. I mean, I'm pretty sure if he met his mate, he'd run away and disappear."

"Maybe, maybe not. I guess we'll see."

Hugh hadn't thought about it before, but he hoped his brothers would find love, too. He wanted all of them to be as happy as he was.

But they would see. Only the future would tell, and for once, Hugh couldn't wait to see that future.

Edward bounced his knee as the elevator went up. He didn't want to be here, but he knew his brother needed him. That was why Henry had sent him to meet Benedict first. He'd wanted to know what Benedict was like and if he was serious about making a deal between their two businesses. Still, it didn't mean that Edward was comfortable with this. He wasn't the one who had this kind of meeting. He was the one who worked behind the scenes, making sure everything was the way he should so that Henry could sweep in and sign deals and do whatever else he did.

There was a reason Henry was the one who'd inherited the business from their father. Henry had been surprised and appalled in the beginning, but it was what Edward and their father had made the decision together. Edward had never wanted to be in Henry's place. He'd never wanted to be the CEO, or to have any kind of power. He enjoyed working for Henry, even though they were brothers, or maybe because of it. He liked making sure that Henry's life was as easy as it could be.

"Stop bouncing your knee," Henry murmured without looking at Edward.

Edward stopped instantly. "Sorry."

"Don't worry about it. You can't show people you're nervous, though. They'll take advantage of it."

Edward didn't think Benedict would, even though he barely knew him, but he nodded anyway. "This is why I'm not the one who makes deals," he murmured.

"You could if you wanted to, but we've already talked about it, and I know what you think. I won't push."

Edward was relieved. He was even more relieved when the elevator pinged and the doors slid open. He stepped out and looked around, searching for Benedict's secretary. He knew she would be the one to greet them, and he smiled at her when she came closer. He tried to remember her name, but he couldn't, so he limited himself to hold his hand out to greet her.

"Good morning," he said.

She smiled back. "Mr. Hunt is waiting for you. If you want to follow me?"

Amanda. That was her name. Edward nodded at her. "Lead the way, Amanda. We'll be right behind you."

Her smile widened as if the fact that he'd remember her name was a good thing. She turned around, and Edward fell into step with her.

He hoped this meeting would go well, and not only because he liked Benedict and Dakota when he'd met them. He knew the odds weren't in their favor, and not only because of Purity. He doubted they would be able to get inside of the building, but he couldn't be sure, and he was afraid, both for himself and for his brother.

But something needed to be done. The elements needed to get closer again. There weren't a lot of them left, although it was hard to say since they didn't mix. Edward was sure of it, though, just like he was sure that if they didn't start to mix, they might disappear entirely. It would be a huge loss, even though humans weren't even aware of their existence.

And of course, Edward wanted to make their father proud, even though he wasn't with them anymore. He wasn't sure this was the best way to do it. He wasn't even sure what his father would think about reuniting the elements the way they'd been before the war. Edward felt that they needed to do it, though. He wasn't a businessman like his brother. He didn't have any kind of power. He didn't want any kind of power. But maybe, in this, he could help.

Amanda stopped in front of the door of Benedict's office and knocked. When he called out to her to enter, she opened the door and stepped aside. "Mr. Hunt? Edward and Henry Long are here."

"Let them in," Benedict answered.

Edward nodded at Amanda as he walked into the office. He wasn't surprised to see that Benedict was behind his desk and that his boyfriend was on the other side of it, but he was surprised to see the other two men in the office. He hadn't expected them, but maybe he should have. They all knew how dangerous this meeting could become if Purity found out about it.

Benedict rose to his feet, already smiling. "Edward. It's a pleasure to see you again," he said, holding his hand out as he walked around the desk.

Edward moved toward him, taking his hand and shaking it. "Same." He stepped aside to introduce Henry. "And this is my brother, Henry. He's the one you'll be having the meeting with. I'm just here for moral support."

Benedict laughed. "It's the same reason I have Dakota with me. It's a pleasure to meet you, Henry. I can call you Henry, right?"

Henry nodded. He was already smiling, and Edward knew he liked Benedict.

Edward cleared his throat and gestured toward the sitting area at the back of the room. "I'll be waiting back there."

Benedict nodded. "As you can see, there are two men here with us today. They're bodyguards, and they work for Dakota. We wanted to be sure nothing would happen during this meeting," he explained. "Alcott is next to the door, while the man in the sitting area is Bay."

Edward gave both of them a smile before turning back to Benedict and Henry. "I'll leave you to your work."

He was relieved that he could step away, but surprised when he sat into one of the armchairs and Bay came closer.

"I'm Bay," he said.

"I'm Edward. Shouldn't you be focused on the meeting?"

"Why should I? It's none of my business."

Edward blinked. "You're a bodyguard. You're supposed to keep your eyes on your clients."

"And right now, you're my client. Benedict will be fine. Dakota isn't looking away from him even for one second. Alcott is focusing on the door, so I don't have to do that, either. You're my only focus until the meeting ends. So, do you want anything to drink? I'm not sure what I can find, but I do know there are coffee and water."

Edward didn't know what to say to that. He wasn't sure what to think about being Bay's only focus. The thought made him wiggle in his seat, and he forced himself to stop and smile blandly at Bay. "Water is fine, thank you."

Bay's smile was more natural. "I'll grab it for you. Wait here."

"I'm not going anywhere unless Edward is, too. Don't worry."

He watched Bay as he walked away. He didn't go far, just off the sitting area, and he opened the closet. Since Edward could only see the back of him, he focused on that, even though he could feel his cheeks heat.

He didn't feel any kind of sexual desire for Bay—or for anyone—but he couldn't deny the man was sexy as hell. He seemed to have a great body under his clothes, and while Edward didn't want to explore it, he wouldn't have minded seeing it. He liked looking at pretty things, and Bay was more than a little pretty.

He pushed those thoughts away. He couldn't afford to think of them. He needed to focus on the meeting and what would come out of it.

He turned toward Henry, but his brother wasn't even looking at him. Why should he have? He was deep in conversation with Benedict, nodding at something Benedict was saying, gesturing when he answered. Edward knew that if he wanted, he could go up to them and become part of their conversation, but why should he? He wasn't part of that world. He probably wouldn't understand half of what they were saying.

His father had tried several times to teach Edward how to step into his shoes when he died or decided to retire. He'd wanted Henry and Edward to work together Edward had never managed to learn. His brain could make sense of the numbers and everything that was necessary to lead the family business, and he'd been more than happy to let Henry take that place. He still was. They worked together, even though they didn't have the same kind of responsibilities.

But he was worried. The deal would put Henry in front of Purity, and it would make a target out of him more than it would of Edward. Edward didn't like it. He knew that talking to Henry about it wouldn't change anything, though. Henry was stubborn, and he thought he was doing the right thing. Edward thought so, too, which was why he wouldn't try to stop his brother.

"Here you go," Bay said. He handed Edward a bottle of water, and Edward took it.

"Thank you."

Bay's smile was sweet. He sat into the armchair next to Edward as if to keep him company. "Don't worry about it."

Edward had to look away so he wouldn't get caught staring.

He had no idea why he was thinking about this kind of

things when it came to Bay. He wasn't attracted to him, not in the sense most people were attracted to other people, but he couldn't deny he was interested.

Bay seemed like an interesting kind of person. Edward didn't know him, so of course, he could be wrong, but he found himself wanting to ask questions, like for example, why he'd become a bodyguard or how working with Dakota was.

He didn't.

He stayed quiet, but he couldn't ignore Bay's presence next to him, not even when he wasn't looking at him. He didn't know why, and he wasn't sure he wanted to find out. What he was sure of was that he was interested in Bay more than he'd been in anyone in a long time, and he wasn't quite sure what to do with that.

ABOUT THE AUTHOR

Catherine is the creator of several series, most of them para-normal, including the Whitedell Pride Series and the Gillham Pack Series. While she graduated in translation, she decided to go the writer's way because it was more fun to create her own stories and characters.

She's been living in Italy for more than twenty years, but she's a daughter of the North—Belgium to be precise—and she misses it so much that she's already planning to move back.

She loves pizza—probably too much—her son, her pets, and of course, books. She sneaks some reading time into her schedule every time she has five minutes free from writing, demands from her various pets and son, and lastly, house-work.

Connect with her:

lievens.catherine@gmail.com

BookBub: https://www.bookbub.com/authors/catherine-lievens

Website: https://authorcatherinelievens.wordpress.com/

Facebook: https://www.facebook.com/catherine.lievens.9

Facebook Group: https://www.facebook.com/groups/411788002341528/

Twitter: https://twitter.com/authorCLievens

Newsletter: http://eepurl.com/c-uvKn

www.ingramcontent.com/pod-product-compliance
Lightning Source LLC
Chambersburg PA
CBHW060633130626

46555CB00002B/786